Bragg's Match

Bragg Brothers # 4

D.E. Haggerty

Also By D.E. Haggerty

Bragg's Truth
Bragg's Love
Perfect Bragg
My Forever Love
Forever For You
Just For Forever
Stay For Forever
Only Forever
Meet Disaster
Meet Not
Meet Dare
Meet Hate
A Hero for Hailey
A Protector for Phoebe
A Soldier for Suzie
A Fox for Faith
A Christmas for Chrissie
A Valentine for Valerie
A Love for Lexi
About Face

Chapter 1

I YAWN AS I shuffle to the kitchen. What a long freaking day. My back aches from sitting behind my pottery wheel for ten straight hours. I stop in front of the refrigerator and raise my hands in the air to stretch out my muscles before I open the door.

"AAAAH!"

I scream at all of the tiny creatures in the fridge staring back at me before I slam the door closed and lean against it to trap whatever's in there.

The front door of the house flies open and Brody freaking Bragg sprints inside. Brody is a new resident in my hometown of Winter Falls. He moved here a few months ago with his brothers.

Since three of his brothers have found love with three of my friends, Brody and I have been hanging out together as the two unattached friends. I thought it was better than being a third-wheel, but now I'm not too sure.

"What's going on?" He doesn't even bother to attempt to hide his smirk.

My body switches from scared out of my mind to irritated in a flash. Brody may be a friend but he's also a prankster who can't be trusted. "What did you do?"

He bats his eyelashes. "What are you talking about?"

I clench my jaw and wave my hand toward the fridge. At least I know there aren't any creatures in there. Just another Brody prank. "You know exactly what I mean."

He smiles. "It's my welcoming gift to you."

"Welcoming gift? Why would you give me a welcoming gift? What are you talking about?"

"I'm your new roomie." He takes a bow.

I cross my arms over my chest. "Roomie? You aren't my roommate."

"Sure, I am." He motions toward the suitcases and boxes near the front door.

"What the hell?" I stomp toward the stuff. "What makes you think you can move in here without discussing it with me first?"

"Crap," he mutters as he runs a hand through his lush hair.

No, not lush hair. Nothing about Brody is lush or beautiful or sexy. Not his sparkling blue eyes I want to drown in. Not his perfect smile with the barest hint of a dimple on his left cheek. Not his broad shoulders that appear strong enough to carry the weight of the world on them.

Okay, fine. He's hot. He's also a man-child. And I'm way too old to be interested in him. No matter what my body thinks. My mind knows better. I don't need another person to look after. I've got enough on my plate as it is.

"Explain." I motion toward the suitcases.

"I think I've been pranked," he mutters.

I slap my hand over my mouth before my laughter can escape. Brody – the prankster to end all pranksters – got pranked? This is precious.

"What happened?" I ask once I manage to get my humor under control.

"My brother, Elder, kicked me out of his house. He said you have room for me."

I can't blame Elder for kicking him out of his house since his wife, Harmony, and her baby niece just moved in with him. Those two deserve their happily ever after considering all the heartbreak my friend Harmony has suffered in her life.

I wish I could find my happily ever after but I've resigned myself to be the best aunt this world has ever seen of the children my friends have.

"Elder didn't discuss you staying here with me." And I will be having words with him.

"I'm not any happier about this than you are. I don't understand why I couldn't stay at Elder's. I sleep on the sofa. I'm not using up any space they need."

I raise an eyebrow. "You want to live with your brother and his family?"

His nose wrinkles. "No, but where else am I supposed to live?"

I cross my arms over my chest. "You could stay at Harmony's place. It's empty now. And I know she offered."

"I'm allergic to dogs."

"You have three brothers. Why can't you live with one of them?"

"Correction. I have four brothers and a half-brother. All of whom are avoiding me."

All of whom are smarter than me. Note to self: Lock my doors from now on.

"How about this? You could – and I understand this is a novel concept for you – find a place of your own?"

His lip curls. "A place of my own?"

"It's simple. You search for a rental house. You sign a lease. You pay your rent. You have a place to live."

He does a mock shiver. "Sounds horrible."

"This is why I don't want you to live here. You're immature and childish."

He scowls. "I'm not a child. I'm thirty-years old."

"And yet you're couch surfing. Real mature."

He smirks. "But I'm done couch surfing now. Rumor has it you have a spare bedroom."

"And you thought putting googly eyes on everything in my refrigerator would be the best way to appeal to me?"

He chuckles. "Got you."

Got me? Is he out of his mind?

"Do you think I want to live with someone who scares the crap out of me on a regular basis?"

He rolls his eyes. "You can't still be mad about the ghost."

"I can't still be mad about the ghost?" I lean forward and hiss at him. "I can be mad about whatever I want to be mad about."

"But I saved you."

"After you scared me half to death dressing up as a ghost and prancing around in front of my living room window."

"Admit it. You thought my ghost was sexy."

"Are you crazy?" He opens his mouth to answer but I throw up a hand to stop him. "No. Don't answer. I don't want to hear it." I blow out a breath. "It's been a long ass day. I don't have the energy to deal with whatever this is right now."

He frowns. "Sit down. Put your feet up. I'll get you something to drink and you can relax."

"I was trying to get something to drink when I opened the fridge to discover it was full of creatures."

He sighs. "I guess you won't be thanking me for my 'thank you for letting me live here' present."

"If this is how you thank people, I want nothing to do with it."

"Understood. No googly eyes on items in the fridge for as long as I'm living here."

I narrow my eyes on him. "I never said you could live here."

"But where else am I going to live?" He pouts.

"Why is this my problem?" I mutter.

I don't know why I'm surprised. I'm the one who's always taking care of everyone's problems. Naturally, his brother and my friend Harmony sent him to me. They knew I'd take care of him. The way I always take care of everyone.

But the last thing I need at the moment is another person to take care of. I'm busy as hell getting ready for the Litha festival in July, which is less than a month away.

This is my busiest season. My small town of Winter Falls attracts tourists from all over during the summer with its festivals. In addition to teaching pottery classes to the tourists, I sell an absolute ton of pottery. I need to make certain I have enough stock available to sell.

And it's not as if I can purchase stock online. No, each piece of pottery I sell is one-hundred percent unique. Between creating the piece, decorating it, firing the clay, glazing, and the glaze fire, I need at least three and a half weeks to create each piece.

Brody grasps my hands and I come out of my reverie. "How can I help you, Soleil?"

His thumbs rub against my inner wrists. My skin warms and goosebumps threaten to break out. Oh no. This can't be happening. I can't be attracted to Brody.

I yank my hands away. "You can help by not pulling stupid pranks to scare the crap out of me."

He shoves his hands in his pockets and rocks back on his heels with a huge smile on his face. "You admit my pranks rock."

"I didn't say—" I cut myself off. I'm not discussing his stupid pranks. "I'm serious. I don't have time for this." I check my watch. "I need to get a few hours of sleep before I get back to work."

"Say no more. I will detain you no longer. Kindly show me where the bedroom I'll be occupying is and I won't bother you any longer."

I frown. "I love how you assume you're going to stay here."

He clutches his chest. "Ah. You love me. I care for you too, Soleil."

"Dork."

I consider my options. I can argue with Brody about him staying here. But I don't have time for his shenanigans. Or I can find him another place to stay. Unfortunately, I can't think of anyone who has room for him right now.

Damn. It appears I have no choice.

"Come on. I'll show you to your room."

"Awesome! You won't regret it."

"I already regret it."

He ignores me. "I'll be the best roommate you can imagine. I don't have parties. Well, except for when my brothers come over for poker night. But don't worry. We won't bother you. I'll plan it on a night when you're out with your girls. And I'll—"

I hold up my hand. I already know he's going to be a terrible roommate. No matter how much he claims to the contrary.

"This is your room." I open the door to my spare bedroom and usher him inside.

He bounces on his toes. "I get a bed. Awesome! Elder, my least favorite brother, didn't give me a bed."

"I need to get some sleep. Try to keep it down," I say as I make my way down the hall.

"Where's your bedroom?"

"I have my own bathroom," I say as I open the door to my bedroom. "You can use the bathroom in the hallway."

"Aw, shucks. Does this mean there's no chance of me bumping into a skimpy robe-wearing Soleil in the hallway?"

His words conjure up thoughts of him sauntering through the hallway with a towel wrapped around his waist. I wonder how those broad shoulders look without a shirt. I wonder…

I cut those thoughts off. There will be no fantasizing about Brody. I have no interest in a man-child who still couch surfs instead of finding his own place to live.

"Sleep tight, roomie. Don't let the bed bugs bite."

"Whatever," I murmur as I shut my bedroom door behind me.

Chapter 2

BRODY

I smile at Soleil as she shuffles into the kitchen.

"Good morning."

She grunts in response. She is not what you would describe as a morning person. I wouldn't be a morning person either if I'd stayed up until 2 a.m. glazing pottery or whatever it is she does in her pottery shed.

"Here you go." I offer her a mug of coffee.

She snatches the coffee from me and drinks big gulps until it's finished. Her eyes fall closed and she sighs. "Exactly what I needed."

I refill the mug. "Do you have an asbestos esophagus?"

Her nose wrinkles and she opens her eyes. Her brown eyes meet mine and I clear my throat before I drown in them. Soleil is one of those rare women who is absolutely gorgeous but completely unassuming. I'm infatuated with her and she thinks I'm a child.

"Why are we discussing asbestos at eight o'clock in the morning?"

I indicate her mug. "Because no normal person could drink scolding hot coffee without burning their esophagus."

She cradles the mug to her chest and smiles. The dimple on her right cheek comes out and I want to taste it with my tongue before placing my mouth against her plump lips as my fingers dive into her shiny brown hair. Is it as soft as silk? How will it feel wrapped around my fist?

My cock stirs and I shut those thoughts down. Soleil would castrate me if she knew what I was thinking about.

"Do you have any idea how late I worked last night? I need this coffee more than I need my next breath."

I know exactly how late she worked last night. I stay up every night and listen for her return from her pottery shed. When I hear her stumble into the house, I get up and check the house is locked up tight before finally going to sleep.

I know it's crazy. We live in Winter Falls. I'm pretty sure the apartment building I lived in back in my hometown of San Diego housed more people than the thousand inhabitants of this small town in Colorado.

But I can't help myself. When it comes to Soleil, I have a driving force to make certain she's safe. I want to care for her – ensure she gets enough rest and has fun – but she's made it perfectly clear she thinks of me as a child.

Too bad for her I love a good challenge. And a challenge wrapped up in the sexy package of Soleil? Irresistible.

"How are your preparations for the festival going?"

She plops down on a kitchen stool. "Okay. I guess." She pushes her hair out of her face and I fist my hands before I reach for those silky strands.

"Do you need help?"

She raises an eyebrow. "Do you know how to fire a kiln?"

"No."

"Glaze pottery?"

"No."

"Wield the pottery wheel?"

"No."

"Then, basically, you're useless to me."

I know she's teasing but those words burn as they pierce my heart. I'm not useless. And I'm not a child. But try convincing my brothers or Soleil otherwise. Not a chance.

"But I am pretty to look at."

I strike a pose with my hip jutted out and my hands under my chin. Heat flares in Soleil's eyes before she blinks and it's gone. But it was there. I saw it. And I won't be forgetting it anytime soon.

She drops her gaze to stare at her coffee. "You're something all right," she mumbles.

"I prefer the words charming, adorable, funny, spontaneous…"

She holds up a hand to stop me. "Too much for early in the morning."

I may not be able to help with her pottery, but there are other ways I can help. "How about breakfast? I can whip up some eggs and bacon."

Her mouth drops open. "You can cook?"

"What's with the surprise? Why wouldn't I be able to cook?"

"I didn't expect you to be able to cook since you spend your life mooching off of your family and friends."

I ignore the sting her words cause and plaster a smile on my face.

"What'll it be? Eggs, bacon? Pancakes?"

She perks up. "Pancakes? You can make pancakes?"

"It's not hard," I say as I begin to gather the ingredients. "You sit there and look beautiful while I get your breakfast ready."

"Beautiful?" She snorts. "I knew you were crazy but I didn't know you were blind, too."

"Beautiful and modest. Great combo."

"Whatever," she mumbles. "Get to making those pancakes before I tell the entire town you're a liar who can't cook."

I clutch my chest. "I can too cook."

I don't touch the liar comment since I've been known to fiddle with the truth on occasion. What can I say? Sometimes a little white lie is necessary. I just hope Soleil doesn't lose her mind when she discovers the truth about my 'allergies'.

After breakfast, Soleil trudges out to her pottery shed in the backyard. I watch to make sure the building doesn't fall down upon her when she shuts the door. To say her shed has seen better days is a massive understatement.

I clean up the kitchen before setting up my computer on the dining room table and getting to work. I'm currently developing a feudal fighting game. It's a passion project I've waited years to work on, but I can't concentrate on swords and crossbows today.

My mind keeps replaying pictures of how tired Soleil appeared this morning. How hard she's working herself all the time. She needs to let loose. Lucky for her, I'm on the case. I'm the perfect person to help her let her hair down. But how?

I give up on the game and save my work as I throw myself into project 'Get Soleil To Loosen Up'. She needs an incentive to kick back. There's no way she'll be relaxing on her own.

I tap my chin as I consider ideas. When nothing springs to mind, I decide to do a bit of recon.

I step outside and tiptoe to Soleil's shed. My ears perk up when I hear music coming from the building. I creep closer until I can peer into the window. Soleil is dancing around the shed while singing as *I Knew You Were Trouble* blares in the background.

Soleil is a Swiftie? I would have never guessed my 'uptight, too busy taking care of everyone else she ends up neglecting herself' woman is a Taylor Swift fan.

This is awesome. I retreat as the perfect plan to cheer Soleil up begins to form in my head. She's going to love this.

I don't need much time to arrange my surprise. Not to toot my own horn, but I am a whiz when it comes to electronics after all.

Once everything's set up, I return to the shed to watch the show. This is going to be wonderful. We'll have a great laugh. Maybe Soleil will fall into my lap. Maybe my lips will accidentally brush hers. Maybe my hands will touch those curves my fingers itch to feel.

My cock perks up. He's extremely interested in the idea of feeling Soleil wrapped around him. I inhale a few deep breaths to calm myself down before I reach the shed and peek in the window.

Soleil is bent over a piece of pottery with what appears to be a turkey baster in her hand. What does she need a turkey baster for?

I check my watch. Time to initiate my Cheer Soleil Up-plan.

Her soft music switches off and the song I chose for her – *The Man* since she's such a Taylor Swift fan – begins.

"Aaaah!"

She screams as the music blares and jumps to her feet. The piece of pottery she was working on totters on the table. Shit. I rush inside but I'm too late.

The pottery is smashed to smithereens on the floor. "Crap."

"Crap?" Her head whips up. "What are you doing in here?"

Her eyes narrow and I can practically see her putting the pieces together in her mind. She points at me. "This is all your fault. Two weeks of work are down the drain because of your stupid prank."

I raise my arms in surrender. "I was trying to get you to relax and have a bit of fun."

She throws her hands in the air. "Have a bit of fun? Does it look as if I have time for a bit of fun?"

"Everyone should make time for fun."

"Not everyone can live off daddy's money," she sneers.

I scowl. I don't live off daddy's money. Did I receive a nice-sized inheritance when my dad died a few years ago? Yes, but I don't live off the money. I invested all of it in *Naked Falls Brewing*, the brewery my brothers, Miller and Elder, own and operate.

I have my own money. Lots of it in fact. But no one knows about it. Probably because I keep it quiet. I'll tell the family when I'm a big success. Not before.

"I'm sorry. I was trying to cheer you up."

Her eyes flash with an emotion I can't read before she blinks and it's gone. "Cheer me up? I don't need cheering up."

She's lying, but now is not the time to call her on it.

"I'll get a broom and help you clean this up."

I whirl around and nearly bump into a shelf of finished pottery.

"STOP!"

I raise my hands and slowly turn toward her. "Nothing happened."

"Nothing happened *yet*." She inhales a deep breath. "Please leave. I do not need your help cleaning up."

"I—"

She cuts me off. "No. I don't want to hear it."

I drop my chin to my chest. "Okay. Fine. I'll go. I'm sorry. I shouldn't have…" I trail off with a shrug.

"No more pranks, Brody!" she shouts after my retreating form.

I make no promises. Pranks are my love language. But maybe next time I'll be a bit more careful because – spoiler alert – she didn't love her surprise.

Chapter 3

What gets wet while drying? A towel! ~ Text from Elder to Brody

I REACH MY ARMS into the air and stretch my back from side to side. Sitting behind a pottery wheel all day is not the best for my back. I should probably attend some yoga classes. I yawn. But who has the time?

I have less than two weeks until the *Litha* festival and I don't have nearly enough pottery pieces ready to sell. Brody breaking a piece last week certainly didn't help.

Brody. He's such a menace. How could he possibly think blaring music would be okay while I'm working on pottery? His idea of cheering a person up and mine are completely different. Where's the wine? The back rub? The snuggling on the sofa?

The snuggling on the sofa? Am I thinking about someone cheering me up or a date? A date with Brody?

Enough with this contemplation. Brody and I are friends and roommates. Nothing more. I need a shower and bed before I fall asleep on my bathroom floor.

I switch on the water before removing my dirty clothes and throwing them in the hamper. I step into the shower and moan as the hot water pounds on my back. This is exactly what I needed.

I wet my hair before pouring shampoo on it. I massage my scalp as I work the shampoo into my hair. I lean back to rinse my hair and—

"Ah! Cold! Cold! Cold!"

I jump out of the shower and wrap a towel around me before rushing out of the bathroom. "Stupid pilot light," I mutter as I hurry down the hallway.

The guest bathroom door flies open and Brody races out. I hold up my hands but I don't have time to stop before I run into him.

Whack!

We smack into each other. Brody wraps his arms around me, pulls me to his chest, and twists as we careen toward the floor. We land with a thud.

As soon as I catch my breath, I start wiggling to get out of his hold. "What are you doing?"

He holds tight to stop my wiggling. "Saving you."

"Saving me? Saving me from what?"

"Hitting your head on the floor."

"I wouldn't have hit my head on the floor if you hadn't run into me. Why weren't you watching where you were going?"

"The water went cold. I thought the pilot light might be out."

My brow furrows. How does he know the water went cold? "The water went cold?"

"Yes. In the shower," he speaks slowly. "Did you hit your head after all?"

"In the shower? You were in the shower?"

"Yes."

"No wonder the water went cold."

"I'm confused."

"My water heater can't handle two people showering at once."

"Lesson learned." He smirks. "On the bright side, we're both naked together in the hallway."

"Naked?" I screech and scramble to my feet. Or, rather, I try to. Brody latches onto my shoulders and I flounder against him. "Let me go! I don't want to be on top of you naked."

"Maybe not. But if you stand up, I'll be exposed."

Oh no. I'm afraid the hardness beneath me isn't Brody's thigh. My nipples tighten and wetness gathers between my thighs.

"Exposed?" I screech to hide my reaction. "Are you a flasher now?"

"I will be if you get off of me."

"Where's your towel? Don't you have a towel? What sane person jumps out of the shower and doesn't grab a towel before racing into the hallway?"

He grins. "Ah, you think I'm sane. You're sweet on me."

"Don't you dare!"

"Dare what?"

"Start with your flirting."

He bats his eyelashes. "Are you saying I'm a good flirt?"

"I'm saying I'm going to knee you in the groin if you don't shut up."

"I hate to point this out. Seriously, I do. But if you knee me in the groin, there's a chance you lose control over the towel straining to stay wrapped around you."

He draws a finger along the edge of the towel and I tremble. No, not tremble. Brody's touch on my body does not make me tremble. I'm shivering is all. I'm wet and it's freezing in the hallway.

I fist my hands before I do something incredibly stupid such as open my towel and see what happens. I have no idea where those thoughts came from. Soleil Hawk does not have sex with men she's not in a committed relationship with.

I blame Brody. Whenever he's around, I suffer from a personality change. Maybe I need to visit a therapist. Or an exorcist.

"Any suggestions on how to get out of this situation without one or both of us exposing ourselves to the other?"

Brody contemplates his answer. "If I promise to keep my eyes closed while you stand up, will you believe me?"

I bark out a laugh. "No."

He smirks. The little shit. "Yeah, I wouldn't believe me either."

I glance toward the open bathroom door. Maybe we can crawl over there together and grab a towel for Brody? But I can't see Brody's towel. I lean forward to get a better look and Brody squeals.

"What?"

He rubs his eyes. "I got your shampoo in my eyes."

"Don't rub your eyes. You need to rinse them."

"Because I have water available to me right now?" He winces. "Fuck. This shit stings. I think I'm going blind."

"You're not going blind. Don't be such a baby."

"Have you had shampoo in your eyes before? It hurts."

I roll my eyes. "Everyone's had shampoo in their eyes before."

He scrunches his eyes closed as tears leak out of them. Shit. He's really suffering. I have no choice.

"Keep your eyes closed."

"I'm not opening my eyes!" he shrieks.

I push myself up and he grunts. I keep my eyes on the bathroom. I will not glance down and check where I accidentally kneed him.

"I'm going to be a blind eunuch before this day is done."

Mystery solved on where I kneed him.

"Yeah, well, you shouldn't be showering this late at night," I grumble as I stand.

As soon as I'm on my feet, I rush to the bathroom and snatch the robe from the back of the door. I step further into the bathroom where I'm out of Brody's view before dropping my towel and putting on the robe. I throw the towel at Brody.

"Cover yourself." I wait until I hear him stand before asking, "Are you decent?"

"Still blind, but decent."

I allow myself to glimpse his way. Phew. His towel is wrapped around his legs and nothing is exposed. Nothing except his chest. Great goddess of pottery Athena. How the hell does

Brody, the prankster who spends his days buried behind his computer, have a six-pack?

My mouth waters as I study his firm muscles. Are they hard to touch? Or is his skin soft? My belly warms as I imagine touching his naked skin. All of his naked skin. Every single inch.

"What's going on?" Brody reaches his hands out to search for me. "Did you desert me here while I'm going blind?"

I wish I could. I'd run away from him and these inappropriate feelings. But I can't let anyone suffer. Not even someone as annoying as Brody Bragg.

"Come on." I grasp his hand and lead him into the bathroom. "I'll rinse your eyes out."

"I got it," he says as he climbs into the shower.

"But the water hasn't warmed up yet."

"A cold shower isn't a bad idea at the moment," he mutters before closing the curtain. The towel comes flying over the top of the curtain rod a few seconds later. Oh my. Brody's naked in the shower.

Don't think about it, Soleil. You have no business thinking about Brody Bragg in your shower. He's an immature prankster who drives you crazy. He's not for you. I back out of the bathroom and shut the door behind me.

I don't know about this whole living together as roommates thing. A roommate has never made me want to rip my towel off and expose myself before.

Chapter 4

I HEAR THE DISTINCT sound of beeping from a truck backing up and bolt upward in bed. The truck sounds awful close to my window. I jump up and rush to the window before pulling aside the curtain.

There's a truck backing up toward my shed. I blink. I must be seeing things. No way is there a truck driving through my yard. But no matter how many times I blink my eyes, it doesn't disappear. What the hell?

I hurry outside. "What's going on?"

The truck stops in front of my shed and Brody jumps out. I should have known. Great. The prankster is at it again. If he breaks another piece of pottery, I'm going to shove him into my pottery kiln. Screw Winter Falls and their peace loving hippy ways. A woman has her limits.

I growl at him. "What are you doing?"

He beams a smile at me. "I'm helping."

"Helping?" I fist my hands on my hips. "I don't want your help. You're a pottery destroyer."

Hurt flashes in his eyes. "I'm trying to make up for my mistake."

"Mistake? How is you blaring music a mistake?"

"I didn't realize how distracting the music would be. I didn't think you'd break any of your pottery."

I blow out a breath. I am done discussing his stupid prank. He can apologize all he wants. Blaring music when someone is working on her art isn't a prank. It's immature and careless.

"Moving on. What are you doing with a truck in my backyard?"

"You said you needed help getting your pottery to the community center for this weekend's festival."

Crap. He's right. I do need help. But I don't trust him with my precious pottery. It's my livelihood. And someone's gotta pay the bills since Brody seems perfectly content to mooch off of me.

"Go on." He shoos me toward the house. "I'll load up while you get dressed."

Get dressed? I glance down at myself and realize I'm standing outside wearing a t-shirt and panties. No shoes. No pants. No bra. No bra? Eek! I cross my arms over my chest. Guessing by the smirk on Brody's face, I'm too late. Damnit. It's not my fault, it's cool outside this morning.

"Be careful or you'll learn firsthand exactly how hot my pottery kiln can get."

He salutes me. "Aye, aye, captain."

I dress as quickly as I can in my 'uniform' aka overalls on top of a t-shirt and a pair of Crocs. Yeah. Yeah. Crocs are ugly. They're also the most comfortable footwear in existence if you're on your feet all day.

I'm still putting my hair into a messy bun as I hurry outside to check on Brody's progress. I swear if he breaks another piece of my pottery, I will kick his ass out of my house. I don't care if he has nowhere else to go. Why is he my problem?

My mouth drops open when I enter my shed. All of the crates with my pottery are gone.

"I finished loading up the crates into the bed of the truck. I figure if we drive real slow, they'll be fine."

Brody pulls his t-shirt up to wipe his brow and I forget about whatever he's saying. I wasn't imagining things the other day. Brody Bragg has a chest sculptors search their entire lives for.

I've never sculpted a thing in my life, but I wouldn't mind using Brody as my test subject. Of course, I'd have to touch all of those muscles first to verify they're real and as hard as they appear.

"Earth to Soleil."

Brody snaps his fingers in front of my face and I whip my head up.

"What?"

"See something you want?" He smirks.

I'm not admitting to anything. Instead, I narrow my eyes on him and feign being annoyed. "You better not get sweat on my pottery."

My pottery can handle sweat perfectly fine. I, on the other hand, am about to combust from imagining how it feels to have Brody's sweaty body gliding against mine.

He grasps the hem of his t-shirt. "No worries. I'll change." He starts to lift the shirt.

"Stop!" I yell. "You're fine."

He winks. "I'm glad you think so."

I roll my eyes. "Laying it on a bit thick, aren't you?"

He waggles his eyebrows. "I know other things that are thick."

Without my permission, my gaze drops to his crotch. Is he thick down there?

No. No. No. Stop this, Soleil. He's too young for you and needs someone to take care of him.

I check my watch. "We should get going."

He chuckles as he places his hand on my lower back and ushers me to the passenger side of the truck. "I like your invisible watch."

At his words, I forget all about the tingling on my back from his touch and glance at my wrist. No watch. I forgot to put it on.

"Whatever," I mumble as he opens the passenger door for me.

"Do you need a lift, pixie?"

I glare at him. I hate being reminded of my height deficiency. "I'm fine."

"You most certainly are."

I growl. "Don't make me kick you in the nuts."

"Kinky."

"You don't have an off switch, do you?"

He leans close to whisper in my ear, "Wouldn't you like to explore and find out?"

I shiver at the feel of his breath along my neck. Damn him. Before I have a chance to make it clear how Soleil and Brody will never be more than roommates, he lifts me up and places me in the seat.

"Buckle up," he orders as he shuts the door and hurries around the front.

"What's this weekend's festival for anyway?" he asks as he switches on the truck and begins driving through the yard.

"I forget you haven't lived in Winter Falls very long and don't know all of our traditions."

He places a hand over his chest. "Ah, you think I fit in."

I lift my chin. "I said nothing of the sort."

"But it's what I heard."

Does he annoy me on purpose? I clear my throat and move on to a safer subject.

"Litha – also known as Midsummer or the Summer Solstice – marks an important transitional moment in the Earth's seasonal cycle. Fertile energy is at its peak and new life is rapidly growing. Seeds have been sown and begin to grow in abundance until Lughnasadh, which is the first harvest."

"I assume luging is another festival." He bounces in his seat. "Do we race down the mountain in a sled?"

"It's Lughnasadh not luging," I correct.

He shrugs. "Doesn't matter what the name is. Knowing Winter Falls, it'll be a blast." He waves to a police officer standing in the middle of the street. "Hey, look, it's Peace."

He stops and rolls down his window. "Hello, half-Bragg, how are you today?"

Peace rolls his eyes. "I'm not a Bragg."

"Thus, the label half-Bragg."

Peace sighs. "Sometimes I wish your brothers never did that genetic test."

He's referring to the genetic test Brody's brothers did that led them to Peace and Winter Falls. Apparently, Brody's dad – Damon Bragg, Sr. – confessed to cheating on his mom when he was on his deathbed. Brody's brother Elder decided to go in search of any possible siblings and discovered Peace is their half-brother.

Brody grins at Peace. "But you love me and my brothers. We're a great addition to your life. Plus, your mom adopted us and there's no take-backs."

Peace ignores Brody to address me. "Good morning, Soleil."

I smile and wave.

"Didn't expect to witness you breaking the Winter Falls' rules today."

Winter Falls' claim to fame is being the first carbon neutral town in the world. One of the ways we keep our carbon footprint small is by banning internal combustion engines such as the engine this truck sports. Most people walk or use the golf carts freely available around town.

"We're not," I claim. "Elder has a permit to have a truck."

"For his brewery business. Not to randomly drive around town."

"Good thing we're not driving around randomly." Brody motions toward the bed of the truck. "We're delivering Soleil's pottery to the community center to sell during the festival."

Peace scans the truck bed. "Sorry, Soleil. I didn't realize." He motions for us to move along.

Brody doesn't move. "Aren't you going to apologize to me?"

"Are you going to stop referring to me as half-Bragg?"

Brody grins. "You want me to lie to you? Shouldn't police officers disapprove of lying?"

Peace runs a hand through his hair. "The Bragg brothers are going to be the death of me." He slaps his hand on top of the truck. "Get moving."

"I'm obviously Peace's favorite brother," Brody says as he resumes driving.

"Wow. I didn't realize you were delusional on top of being a prankster."

"I prefer the word visionary or forward thinking."

"Delusional."

"No, you're confused. I mean…" He slows the truck to a stop in the middle of the street and gestures to a man. "Do you see a man not wearing any pants walking two squirrels on a leash or am I seeing things?"

I giggle. "It's Forest, the pet store owner. Surely, you've seen him galivanting around town before?"

He shakes his head as we begin driving again. "I need to get out more."

I point to the alley leading to the community center. "Turn here. We can't drive through Main Street with the street fair being set up."

He pulls to a stop behind the center and jumps out before rushing to open my door. "My lady." He offers me his hand.

I ignore how a spark ignites when our hands touch. It's static electricity is all. There's not a spark between me and Brody Bragg. Nope. No way. Can't be. For good measure, I yank my hand away.

"Where do you want the crates?" he asks as he lowers the truck's tailgate and picks up the first one.

"Let me show you." I hurry to open the door and usher him inside.

With Brody's help, we get the truck unloaded in less than fifteen minutes. All the crates are now scattered around the floor in the room I use to teach classes to visitors during festivals. I study the mess. I'll need more than fifteen minutes to get everything arranged.

"Do you want me to stay and help you set up?" Brody asks.

"No!" I scream as an image of the pottery I dropped when he pranked me flashes in my mind. Several people glance in our direction. I clear my throat. "I mean no, thank you."

"Alrighty then. I'll be back this evening to help you."

I open my mouth to argue with him but he waves and strolls away before I get the chance. I don't watch his spectacular ass as he leaves. And I certainly don't wonder if his ass is as muscular as his chest.

Nope. Not I. I have no interest in a prankster who doesn't act his age. I don't need another person I have to take care of. I want someone who will take care of me.

Chapter 5

I BARELY MANAGE TO get the door open of *Fall Into A Good Book*, the bookstore in Winter Falls, for this month's smutty book club meeting before my friend Ashlyn attacks me.

"And? Have you and Brody groped for trout in a particular river?" She waggles her eyebrows.

The rest of my friends – Moon, Eden, and Harmony – gather around me. The curiosity is clear to see in their eyes. Snooping into each other's business is one of the main pastimes of Winter Falls. Secrets have no place in this small town.

I scowl at them. "We're here for book club."

"Attending smutty book club and discussing your sex life are not mutually exclusive," Harmony claims.

Sex life? What sex life?

"No baby?" I pout when I notice her arms are empty.

Harmony recently gained custody of her cousin's daughter when her cousin passed away. Brody's brother, Elder, stepped up to help her out and now the two are married and blissfully in love. And I'm not jealous at all.

Okay, fine. I'm a tiny bit jealous. I want love and babies. Considering I live in a small town and never plan to leave Winter Falls, my love ship may have sailed and it doesn't appear to be making a return voyage.

Harmony wags her finger at me. "Elder's watching him and you're not changing the subject."

Ashlyn forces her way back to the front of the group. She's a bit of an attention hog. "Exactly. Has Brody assaulted you with a friendly weapon?"

I purse my lips. "No one's assaulting anyone."

"My audiobooks are more fun than this," she complains before whirling away. "I'm getting a drink."

Ashlyn is a well-known audiobook narrator who specializes in steamy romance. She even has her own studio in town, *Bertie's Recording Studio.* Thanks to the success of her studio, it's not unusual to bump into a famous singer or band member strolling through town.

"Good. She's gone. You can tell us the truth now," Moon whispers. "We won't say a word to her."

Moon is full of it. She's been best friends with Ashlyn since the two met in kindergarten. They don't keep secrets from each other. As if anyone in Winter Falls would know what a secret is anyway.

"There's nothing to tell."

And there isn't. Have I maybe stared at Brody's body a time or two? Yes. But there's nothing wrong with staring at pretty things. I am an artist after all. Pretty things are my bread and butter.

"Come on," Moon cajoles. "I've got the Bragg woman t-shirt sitting in my shopping cart waiting for me to press buy."

Exactly why I'm not telling her about the shower incident. "Just because you fell in love with a Bragg brother doesn't mean—"

Eden clears her throat.

"Correction. Just because you, Eden, and Harmony have fallen in love with Bragg brothers doesn't mean I will."

I know it sounds crazy but three of my best friends have fallen in love with brothers. Moon was the first to fall. She's in love with Riley who happens to be Brody's identical twin. After her, Eden fell for Miller. And, finally, Harmony's with Miller's fraternal twin, Elder.

I'd say I don't know how Mrs. Bragg handled having five sons, including two sets of twins, but I would love to have five children. I've dreamed of having a big family ever since my mom got sick and I realized I'd always be an only child.

"Why not fall in love with a Bragg brother?" Eden asks. "We know you want a family."

Of course, they know. I said it before and I'll say it again – there are no secrets in Winter Falls.

"And Brody's hot," Moon adds.

I roll my eyes. "You don't get a vote since your man, Riley, is Brody's identical twin."

She shrugs. "It doesn't mean it isn't true."

Eden sighs. "Personally, I think Miller is the hottest of the Brody bunch."

"How her tune has changed. Last year you would have gladly torn Miller's arm off and beat him with it," Harmony reminds her.

Eden waggles her eyebrows. "I've got better things to do with his arms now."

"Personally, I think their whole enemies thing was foreplay," Moon says.

While they're distracted, I inch backwards. My friends mean well. I know they do. They want me to be happy and in love the way they are. I want to be in love, too! But not with Brody Bragg. He's too immature for me.

"There you are."

I whirl around to confront the person. Shit. It's the gossip gals. And they're surrounding me. Amateur mistake. Always know where the gossip gals are at all times. The gossip gals – Feather, Petal, Sage, Cayenne, and Clove – are elderly women who think it's their duty to matchmake all of the single people in town. In other words, they're a menace.

"I heard you're living with Brody Bragg now," Sage says.

Sage is the 'leader' of the gossip gal gang and the one you need to watch out for the most. She works as the police dispatcher and doesn't hesitate to use any of the information she learns at the police station to her own advantage.

"I'm not living with Brody. He's sleeping in my spare room until he finds somewhere to live."

They don't need to know how, ever since the shower incident, he wanders around the house without a t-shirt as often as he can. I swear he stands in the bathroom waiting for me to enter the hallway before sauntering out with the smallest towel possible wrapped around his waist. Judging by how he smirks as he strolls past me, I'm right.

"I'll have some candles wrapped up for you," Petal says.

Petal owns *Sensual Scents*, the candle store in town. Except it's not a normal candle store. She specializes in 'erotic' candles as in massage candles and candles for wax play. None of those usual pretty smelling candles for her. Although her massage candles do smell nice.

I hold up my hand. "I don't need any candles."

"Are you not into wax play?" she asks.

I've never tried wax play. I've never had a sexual partner I trusted enough to give it a go. The image of Brody dripping wax onto my bare breasts pops into my mind and I have to lock my muscles before a full body shiver overcomes me. Brody is not a candidate in the 'first man I try wax play with' contest.

Cayenne studies me. "You could consider returning to yoga. Yoga is great for improving your sex life."

Cayenne used to own the yoga studio, *Earth Bliss*. Peace's fiancée, Olivia, operates the studio now. Knowing Olivia, she'd jump at the chance to teach some sexy yoga class, which is why I am never mentioning this conversation to her.

Clove smiles. "I knew the Bragg brothers were going to be a great addition to Winter Falls."

I raise an eyebrow. "Which is why you ran Elder out of *Clove's Coffee Corner* when he first arrived in town."

She scowls. "He asked where the nearest *Starbucks* was. He's lucky I didn't chase him out of my coffee shop with a wooden spoon."

"I have the perfect book," Feather says. Although Feather owns the ice cream store in town, *Feather's Frozen Delights,* she's better known for her self-appointed position as book picker outer for the smutty book club.

"What book?" Sage asks before I have a chance to say I don't need a book.

"*The Wild Card* by Cassie-Ann L. Miller."

My eyes narrow on Feather. I've read *The Wild Card.* I don't need to be a genius to figure out why she's suggesting that particular book.

"No. I'm not reading a book with a hero who's seven years younger than the heroine." Besides, Brody's eight years younger than me, I think, but know better than to say.

Feather purses her lips. "Are you prejudiced against younger men?"

"I don't think it's prejudiced to prefer a mature man."

"Brody's a grown man," Feather insists.

I snort. "A grown man who thinks it's okay to prank someone and make them shit his pants."

I'm not exaggerating. Brody pranks his brothers all the time. He considers it a sign of prowess when he manages to get one of his brothers to lose control of their bowels. What he dubs prowess, I consider childish.

"This is going to change the odds calculations," Sage grumbles.

I clench my jaw. One of Winter Falls' favorite past times is betting. The residents will bet on anything from what the lunch special at the diner will be to the latest matchmaking project of the Gossip Gals.

I sigh. "I'm sorry to disappoint you ladies, but there will be no winning of any bets about me and Brody since we will never be a couple."

Sage barks out a laugh. "You wouldn't believe the number of times someone has said the very same thing to me. Guess what?" She winks at me. "They always end up eating their words."

"There's a first time for everything," I sing as I walk away.

I eye the rear exit. I could sneak out. If the gossip gals have their sights set on matching me and Brody, it's not safe to be out in public. Who knows what tricks they'll get up to?

Ashlyn moves to stand in front of the rear exit. She crosses her arms over her chest and raises an eyebrow in challenge. Dang it. Ashlyn's seven inches taller than me. There's no way I can escape with her around.

I make my way to the temporary bar instead. Maybe if I drink enough wine, I won't want to attack the next person who claims Brody is my match.

Have they not met him? Brody is most definitely not my match.

Chapter 6

BRODY

"Are you ready to lose your undies?" I ask when I enter Elder's house for our monthly Bragg poker night.

My brothers – Riley, Miller, and Elder as well as my half-brother Peace – are already here. Our oldest brother, Damon, is missing since he didn't move to Winter Falls when the rest of us relocated here from our hometown of San Diego. Which is probably for the best since Damon is a total fuddy-duddy.

Miller snorts. "Our undies?"

"Oops! I forgot. Big brother grump thinks wearing underwear will shrink his tiny dick and make it even smaller."

Miller growls as he steps toward me. I chuckle and hide behind Riley. "You're my twin. You have to save me."

Riley pushes me away. "There are no rules about saving my twin when he's being an idiot and poking the bear."

I tap my chin as I pretend to study Miller's appearance. "Miller does kind of remind me of a bear."

Miller smirks. "At least this bear is getting some on the regular, unlike some boys."

I ignore his dig at my age. "Tell us more. Does Eden enjoy it when you tie her up?"

Miller steps toward me and I cackle. He's too easy to rile up. It's not a challenge. I need a challenge. I glance around the room.

Elder wags his finger at me. "Don't you dare start with me. I'm not in the mood."

"Ah. What's wrong, big brother? Does Billy the goat not love you anymore? Poor guy."

Elder's wife, Harmony, is a total animal nut. She works at the Wildlife Refuge outside of town. She also keeps three dogs and a goat as pets. The goat and Elder do not get along. Probably because the goat French kissed Elder at their initial meeting and my brother isn't one to let a thing such as an uninvited kiss go.

"Billy the goat likes me just fine."

I clutch my chest. "But he doesn't love you anymore. I'm sorry for your heartbreak."

Elder smirks. "Speaking of heartbreak, how are things with Soleil going?"

I feign nonchalance. "Fine. She gave me my own room. Unlike my flesh and blood brother who made me sleep on the couch."

"Because you were supposed to find your own place to live and not camp out on my sofa for your entire life."

"Yeah, bro," Riley adds. "Maybe you should get a real job. Where you earn real money. Money to pay rent."

Miller grunts in agreement.

I swallow my scowl. I have a real job. In fact, I have my own company. My own company with a net worth of several million dollars.

But my brothers don't know about my company. And I'm not telling them until I've made a success of it. But when I do? I'm going to rub it into their faces. I can't wait.

"I thought you had a job as a computer programmer," Peace says and I want to hug him. I won't, but I want to.

Riley snorts. "He 'freelances', which basically means he's lazy and doesn't want a job to tie him down."

I wouldn't refer to working sixty plus hours a week as lazy, but I let Riley's comment slide. If I correct him now, I'll have to explain and I'm not ready to explain. Not yet.

I rub my hands together. "Who's ready to get their ass kicked in poker?"

"If you cheat again, I'm tying you to the flagpole in front of the high school in your underwear," Miller grumbles.

"Moi? Cheat? Never."

I don't cheat. Not exactly. Do I play pranks in the middle of the game to distract other players? Maybe. But it's not my fault if they get easily distracted.

Miller crosses his arms over his chest. "And you didn't try to use marked cards the last time we played?"

"I didn't use them, though, did I? Therefore, you can't complain about my cheating."

I sit at the dining room table, which is all set up for our poker game. "What a good looking table, Elder."

"It's nice I can finally see it since your work is no longer in a mess on top of it."

I'm a bit of a messy worker. Truth be told. I should probably get an office and an assistant. I can't keep up with the gazillion tasks of managing a company on my own while also handling most of the software coding for the games we develop.

Everyone sits at the table and Elder hands out beers. I read the label *Ale Your Clothes Off*. I chuckle before trying the beer.

"This is good. Is it a new recipe?" I ask.

My brothers, Miller and Elder, in addition to being fraternal twins – which isn't really twins in my opinion – own and operate *Naked Falls Brewing* together here in town. From what I understand, there was a ton of resistance from locals when they arrived a few years ago to set up the brewery, but now they're settled in town and both of their girlfriends are locals. The Bragg bunch is here to stay!

Miller grunts at my question.

"I thought Eden was training him to talk," I say.

"I'm not a fucking dog," Miller growls.

"Oh look! It's working. He's talking again."

Riley sighs. "You're dying for him to smack you, aren't you?"

I shrug. "He can try."

"Enough of this small talk," Elder says. "I want to know what Brody's going to do about Soleil."

My brow furrows. "About Soleil? Soleil isn't a problem to be solved."

"But the tent in your pants whenever she's around is definitely a problem," Riley says and my brothers laugh.

"I can't help it my dick is too big to be hidden in my pants."

"Soleil's always wanted a family," Peace chimes in.

A ball of something unpleasant forms in my stomach. It annoys me how my half-brother knows more about the woman I'm infatuated with than I do. I want to know all of Soleil's secrets – how does she taste, how does she look when she comes, how heavy are her breasts.

My cock starts to harden in my pants and I shut those thoughts down before my situation becomes evident to my brothers. I'd never hear the end of it if I got a hard-on from talking about a woman during a poker game.

Elder chuckles. "Can you imagine Brody with a family? He's a baby himself."

"Hey now. I'm thirty. I'm not a baby."

He ruffles my hair. "You'll always be a baby to me."

I glare at him. "Says the man who almost ruined the best thing to ever happen to him because he was afraid to have children."

Elder's smile stretches from ear to ear. "Harmony and my baby girl, Robin, are definitely the best things to happen to me."

"Personally, I'm betting on Soleil never giving Brody the time of day," Riley says.

"What the hell? Where's the twin support?"

"I call it like I see it and Soleil has no interest in you."

He's wrong. I've seen the interest flare in Soleil's brown eyes. I've heard her breath catch when we touch and sparks ignite. She's interested, but she's resisting me because she thinks I'm too young for her. What do our ages matter when Soleil was put on this earth for me?

"Any news on our alleged other brother?" I ask Peace.

I actually don't care to meet yet more children dear old dad conceived out of wedlock but I also don't want to discuss Soleil anymore. I have no desire to argue with my brothers about whether or not she'll give me a chance. She will. You can count on it.

"Nothing." Peace frowns. "I don't get it. It's almost as if he's in witness protection. It's as if he dropped off the face of the earth."

"Is there anyone you can contact to confirm if he's in witness protection?"

"The US Marshalls aren't exactly blabbing when it comes to who's in witness protection."

"We're at a dead end?"

"I think we are."

"Now back to our regularly scheduled program of teasing Brody about his crush on an older woman," Elder says.

"Nothing wrong with an older woman," I say.

"Except this particular older woman has no desire to play hide the sausage with you," Riley says.

I wiggle my eyebrows. "Because she hasn't seen how big my sausage is yet."

Something crashes into the sliding glass door behind the dining room table. About damn time.

"Ah, shucks. Is it Billy coming to visit his boyfriend?" I don't bother trying to hide the humor in my voice.

Elder stands and marches to the door. "What the hell did you do to Billy?"

"*I* didn't do anything. Billy told me he's a princess, so I made sure he had the appropriate clothes."

Elder opens the door and Billy strolls in the house wearing a tiara and pink boa. The goat buts his horns against Elder's legs.

"Ah look. He missed you."

Elder glares at me. "I'm going to kill you."

I spring from my chair. "You have to catch me first."

I scramble out the front door of the house knowing Elder can't follow me or he'll risk the goat coming with and getting lost. Harmony would kill him if her goat got lost. Although how hard can it be to find a goat wearing a tiara?

Chapter 7

I SCOWL WHEN I enter the living area and notice the kitchen table is completely covered in papers. I fist my hands on my hips and yell, "Brody!"

He swaggers down the hallway wearing a pair of shorts slung low on his hips and nothing else. I can't help but drink in the sight of him. My fingers itch to reach out and touch those abs to discover how they feel. With a tiny bit of effort, those shorts could be out of my way. My body heats as I imagine licking every inch of his skin.

"Is there something you need?"

A cold shower? I clear my throat. "Where are your clothes?"

He holds up his t-shirt. "I was getting dressed when you rang, my liege." He bows in front of me.

"You do realize liege is a term from feudal society and refers to the unconditional bond between a man and his overlord."

He wiggles his eyebrows. "Am I the man or the overlord?"

I open my mouth to respond but I snap it shut again. This is a stupid conversation. I motion to the table instead. "Why is there a mess on my kitchen table?"

"One." He holds up a finger. "It's *our* kitchen table." He holds up another finger. "And, two, this is not a mess. This is my work."

I grit my teeth. It is not *our* kitchen table. He's a guest in my house. Nothing more.

"Can you put your work elsewhere? I eat on my kitchen table."

"Okay."

He saunters toward the door and I don't sigh when he puts on his t-shirt to cover up his shoulder muscles. Who knew shoulders were sexy? I inhale a deep breath and force my thoughts back to the matter at hand.

"Where are you going? The table is in the opposite direction."

"Harmony and Elder's housewarming party."

Now I'm grinding my teeth. "Aren't you going to clean this mess up first?"

He checks his watch. "No time. I do hate to be late."

I scowl. He's full of shit. He's never on time. "Liar."

He clutches his chest. "Ah, you like me." He motions to the door. "Come along. If you're nice, I'll let you accompany me to the party."

I stare at the mess on the table for another second before I give in. There's no sense trying to change Brody's mind now.

"Accompany you to the party?" I mutter as we walk out the door. "What's with all the old-fashioned language?"

"I'm working on a feudal fighting game for a client."

"A feudal fighting game? What's a feudal fighting game?"

"It's really cool." His hands fly in the air as he explains. "It's a fighting game where strategy trumps fighting techniques. You have tactics such as maintaining unity in morale, misleading troop movements to surprise opposing armies, spreading misinformation regarding army size and provisions, and, naturally, there's raiding."

"Sounds violent."

"But it's not because it's all about strategy."

I shrug. I have no interest in videogames no matter how much I enjoy watching Brody's blue eyes sparkle with interest as he explains.

We arrive at Elder and Harmony's house and I walk inside where I join my friends Moon, Riley, Harmony, Eden, and Miller who are gathered in the living room.

"The Bragg bunch is impossible!" Moon shouts before I can greet anyone.

She is not wrong. "I'm with Moon."

"I am not impossible," Brody claims.

He's completely impossible. "You made me drop my pottery."

"I didn't mean to. It was an accident."

Accident? Does he know what the word means?

"You blaring music loud enough to wake the dead was an accident?" I snarl at him.

Elder arrives with baby Robin in his arms. "What was an accident?"

"Nothing!" I yell since it wasn't an accident.

Eden wiggles her hands at Elder. "Give me the baby."

Elder tightens his hold on Robin. "No. Get your own baby."

Miller growls and Eden pats his middle until he calms down. "Yes, your brother is a dickhead but he didn't mean to be insensitive."

"Didn't mean to be insensitive?" Harmony glances between Miller and Eden. "Are you two trying?"

Eden's cheeks darken. "No success yet but we're trying."

I ignore the ball of jealousy trying to form in my stomach. I refuse to be jealous of my friends.

Harmony claps. "Robin will have a cousin to play with."

My phone vibrates in my pocket before the song *Call me maybe* begins to play. A song I cannot stand. A song Brody knows I cannot stand.

I point my finger at him. "I'm going to kill you in your sleep."

He laughs. "You can't kill me if you can't catch me." He runs off and I give chase.

"Where are you going?" I ask as he races down the hallway. "This is a dead end."

He opens a door and rushes in. I scramble inside before he can shut me out.

"I'm serious, Brody. You have to stop with all of these pranks," I say as I prowl after him.

"What's the big deal? It's just a song."

"A song you know I hate."

His eyes sparkle with mirth as he backs up.

"Where are you going to flee to now?" I open my arms wide to indicate the room we're in. It's the nursery. There's nowhere to hide in here.

He straightens his back. "Who says I'm fleeing?"

"Everyone who saw you speed down the hallway with me chasing after you."

He smirks. "Got you to chase me, didn't I?"

I narrow my eyes on him. "You want me to chase you? What are you up to now?"

Brody and his stupid pranks. He's going to give me a heart attack one of these days. I still have nightmares about the time he dressed up as a ghost and scared me half to death. I nearly peed my pants in fright.

"This." He shackles my wrist and whirls me around until my back is plastered against the wall and he's looming over me.

"What are you doing?" I scan the room. "Is a skeleton going to pop out from underneath Robin's cot?"

"No skeletons but I do have some bones I wouldn't mind discussing."

He punches his hips and his hard length hits my belly. Sparks ignite in my stomach and travel down to my core.

I gasp. "What are you doing?"

He tucks a strand of hair behind my ear. "I'm making my move."

"Making your move?" I narrow my eyes on him. "Is this some kind of dare? Are your brothers behind this?"

He scowls. "My brothers have nothing to do with this."

"I don't get it." I don't want to get it, is closer to the truth.

"What's there to get? You're a beautiful woman. I'm attracted to you."

He's made his attraction perfectly obvious and I've become a champion at ignoring his innuendos. Unfortunately, it sounds as if he's done being discreet. I need to shut this down.

"I'm also old enough to be your mother."

He rolls his eyes. "You're eight years older than me."

"In biological years."

"Are there other years than biological years?"

"Yes." I nod. "Maturity years."

"I'm mature. I'm an adult."

"An adult who thinks it's funny to make someone shit their pants in fright."

He chuckles. "Come on. It was hilarious when the air horn went off and Elder lost control of his bladder."

"This is exactly what I mean. You're a child."

He punches his hips against my stomach again and those darn sparks ignite. "I am not a child," he grits out.

"Being able to maintain an erection doesn't change your emotional age."

"Found them!" Sage exclaims as the door bangs open.

"Oh my." Feather waves a hand in front of her face.

"Yeah," Petal squeals. "This is going to be my all-time favorite project."

"What are we going to name this one?" Clove asks.

"Project Cub obviously." Cayenne motions toward us.

Project Cub? More proof I'm too old for Brody. I shove him away and make my way toward the door.

"Good luck with your little project," I say as I push past the gossip gals.

They won't be getting any help from me. Brody is way too young and immature for me. I have enough trouble taking care of my friends. I don't need another person to mother. And I certainly don't want a significant other who needs mothering.

"It's a challenge. I do love a challenge," Sage says.

"Challenge accepted!" Brody shouts.

Great. I think I waved a flag at the bull. The bull who's living in my house. Never mind. Bullfighting can't be too difficult. I know how to knit. I'll have a red cape knitted in no time. See if Brody dares to come near me then.

Chapter 8

BRODY

I slap the bar. "Bartender, hit me."

Cassandra, the lovely bartender at *Electric Vibes* – the one and only bar in Winter Falls, pours another shot of tequila into my glass.

"Do you want me to do the whole bartender thing where I pretend to worry about what's wrong with you? And ask you all kinds of intrusive questions?"

"Nope. I'm fine. Absolutely fine. Nothing going on here."

She sighs. I guess I oversold it.

"What's wrong, Brody? Love got you down?"

"Ha! Love! What's love got to do with it?"

"So, it's definitely love."

"What do I know about love? I'm a child," I snarl.

"Aren't you thirty?"

I dismiss her comment with a wave of my hand. My barstool wobbles with the movement, and I have to catch myself before I fall. I've probably had enough tequila. Oh, who am I kidding? You can never have enough tequila!

I mimic the sound of Soleil's voice. "It's not my biological age. It's my emotional age."

"Your emotional age?" Her brow furrows. "Don't you control your emotional age?"

I stare at Cassandra. She's a little fuzzy. I narrow my eyes and try it again. Nope. Still fuzzy.

"What do you mean?"

"I mean you can change your emotional intelligence. There must be some book explaining it all."

"Book? What an excellent idea!"

I stand. The room spins and I grab hold of the bar before the spinning room can carry me away to a faraway land where vampires suck my blood.

"Excuse me. I have places to be."

"Aren't you going to drink your shot?"

"It's tequila," I say as if that's an answer. Because it is. I can't resist the yummy taste of tequila. Can anyone? I grab the shot and down it. Yep. Yummy.

"Later!"

I head for the door and run straight into a chair. I move it but another one appears in its place. Where the hell are all of these chairs coming from? I manage to kick them out of my way and make it to the door.

Now, where is the library again? Ah yes, on the town square. I turn toward the square.

Yowzah! The temperature has risen by several degrees while I was inside the bar. It is hot out here. I'm wearing entirely too many clothes.

I whip my t-shirt off before pushing down my pants. Oops! I should have taken off my shoes first. I toe off my shoes and kick off my pants. Hold on. The briefs need to go as well. Ah, much better.

I abandon the clothes on the ground where they fall. No time to worry about them when I have a library to break into.

Can you actually break into a library? I don't think you can. After all, all the books inside are free to borrow. Libraries should be open all the time, so when you have a book emergency you can grab what you need.

I'll suggest this at the next town meeting. I'm certain everyone will agree with me. I'm a genius.

I reach the library and try the front door. Huh. It's locked. I bang on it but it doesn't open and no one comes running to assist me with my book emergency.

No worries. I'll climb in through a window. I'm excellent at climbing through windows.

I bound down the stairs and round the building. I stop when I discover a window at shoulder height. Perfect.

"Brody Bragg, what are you doing?"

I whirl around. I wave when I recognize my half-brother. "Hey, Peace! Can you give me a boost?"

"Brody."

"Peace. Why are we saying each other's names? Is this some kind of game? Am I winning?"

He huffs. "Brody, what do you notice about the clothes I'm wearing?"

I scrunch up my nose. "Why are you wearing clothes? It's hot outside. I wouldn't wear any clothes if I were you."

"It's raining."

I glance up and drops of rain hit me in the face. "You are correct, sir. It is raining. Give the man a badge for his observation skills." I clap.

Peace clears his throat. "I meant. Did you notice I'm wearing my uniform?"

I squint at him. Yep, he's in uniform all right. Peace is a police officer in Winter Falls. I chuckle. It never fails to amuse me how a man named Peace is a peace officer.

"And, because I'm in uniform, I'm on duty."

"Ah, gotcha. You don't have time to give me a boost. Never mind, officer. Off you go." I wave him away and return to the dilemma of how to open the window.

I study it. I bet if I push hard enough, it'll open. Easy peasy.

I lift my hands, but someone grabs my wrist and pulls me away. I bat the person away.

"Oh, it's you, Peace. I thought you left."

"You thought I left?"

"Duh. You're working. I understand you don't have time to help me. I won't hold it against you."

He drags me away from the window. I yank my hand out of his hold. "What are you doing?"

"I'm ensuring you don't commit a crime on my watch."

"Commit a crime? What crime would I be committing?" I glance down at my body. "Is it because I'm naked?"

"You were literally trying to break into the library in front of me."

"You can't break into a library. Libraries are for the people." I pound my chest with a fist before raising it in the air.

"Nevertheless. I'm going to have to issue you a formal warning."

"A formal warning? I'm your brother. You wouldn't issue me a warning, would you?"

Peace rubs a hand down his face. "I'm issuing you a warning because you're my brother."

"Pig! You're issuing me a warning because I'm your brother! What the hell?"

"Don't call me a pig," he growls.

I lean close to yell in his face. "Pig!"

"Your warning is now a night in jail."

"Ha! You can't arrest me if you can't catch me."

I race down the street. "Peace is arresting me!" I shout. "He's embarrassed because my dick is bigger than his!"

"Stop shouting!" Peace yells at me as he chases me.

"Why? Are you afraid the whole town will hear about how my dick is bigger than yours?"

"I'm not—"

I wheel around to jog backwards. "You're not what?"

"I'm not discussing the size of my dick with you."

"Ah, is Peace embarrassed about the size of his dick?"

"Can you stop running?"

I snort. "And let you arrest me with your tiny dick? I think not."

"I don't have a tiny dick."

"Prove it!"

"Stop trying to wake everyone in town."

I roll my eyes. "What are you going to do about it, pig?"

"I'm going to arrest you for that."

"Not if you can't catch me," I taunt before sprinting away.

"Don't make me chase you."

"Ah, is Peace afraid his younger brother is faster than him?"

I glance back over my shoulder to see if he's catching up. He's puffing hard. Ick. I feel something wet on my foot and look down. It's mud. Why is there mud in the street? Oh yeah, it's raining.

Suddenly, I'm on my back in the street. "What happened?"

"You slipped in the mud."

"Crap. No fair."

"And making me chase your naked ass through Main Street was fair?"

"You didn't have to chase me," I say as I stand.

He shackles my wrist. Literally. There's now a handcuff on it.

"What are you doing?"

He finishes handcuffing me and drags me toward the police station.

"Arresting you."

"But I didn't do anything wrong."

"You tried to break into the library, called a police officer a pig, and resisted arrest."

"I didn't resist arrest," I argue because it's possible I might have done the two other things he mentioned.

"You ran from a police officer."

"And?"

"Running from an officer of the law is resisting arrest."

I sigh. "Is this because you're jealous of how big my dick is?"

"Can you stop talking about your dick for one minute?"

"I can. But you should probably talk to a therapist about your small dick syndrome."

"I do not have small dick syndrome," he grumbles.

"Of course, you don't. And I don't want a woman who thinks I'm a child."

"What did you say?"

"Nothing. Go ahead, officer. Book me."

Chapter 9

MAN, I'M TIRED. I can barely keep my eyes open as I drag myself from my pottery shed into the house. I blame Brody for how tired I am.

Trying to sleep when the man you know wants you is sleeping two doors away is not easy. A man who has six-pack abs, a firm ass, and broad shoulders. A man who—

Nope. *Not a man, Soleil.* He's a child. And I don't need another person to take care of. I want someone to take care of me for a change.

Plus, I don't have sex with men I'm not committed to. Ever. No exceptions. Not even for a man whose cock felt long and hard against my stomach.

I shove all the sexy thoughts out of my mind and force myself to shower before throwing on a t-shirt and crawling into bed. I close my eyes and—

Boom!

My eyes fly open and I jump out of bed. What was that noise? Was it an explosion?

Creak!

My heart stalls in my chest. The sound is coming from inside the house. I grab the baseball bat next to my door before I crack it open and peek around the corner. The hallway's dark making it impossible to see if anyone's lurking there waiting to attack me.

I inhale a deep breath before stepping out of my room and starting to creep toward the living room.

Bam!

The crash came from behind me. I whirl around and sprint toward it. There's another banging sound and I hone in on it. It's coming from Brody's room. Is he being attacked? I hold my bat up and square my shoulders before kicking the door open.

"I got you!" I yell as I enter.

"I didn't do it, officer!" Brody holds up his hands.

"Brody? What are you doing in here?"

"This is my bedroom."

"I mean…"

I pause to scan the room. My eyes nearly bug out of my head when I notice his bed is destroyed. Totally and completely destroyed. The headboard is in pieces on the floor and the mattress appears black and singed. I sniff.

"Do I smell fire?"

"Not fire exactly."

"What's going on in here?"

He motions to me. "Can you drop the bat before I explain? I admit I screwed up but beating me with a bat is a bit excessive, don't ya think?"

I use the bat to indicate what used to be a bed. The bed I paid for. Not *his* bed. "I'm not the one who's being excessive."

He drops his hands. "It was an accident."

"An accident? Like oops, I started my bed on fire and the resulting explosion broke the headboard and frame?"

"Exactly." He grins.

I can't believe him. He's actually grinning. Does he think this situation is funny? There is nothing funny about this situation. I stalk toward him and poke his chest.

"I hope you're happy with yourself. You've now destroyed your bed. I guess you'll have to find somewhere else to live."

And now it might be me who's grinning at an inappropriate moment. This is actually perfect. It sucks Brody ruined my spare bed but I'm willing to sacrifice some furniture to get him out of my house. There's a limit to how long I can resist temptation and Brody spells temptation in all caps with flashing neon lights.

Brody rears back. "Why would I move out?"

I indicate the ruins of the bed. "You have nowhere to sleep."

"But I have nowhere to go."

"Dude, you have three brothers and a half-brother who live in town. And your mother lives in town, too. You have options."

"First of all, ew. I'm not moving in with my mom. She's living with Lennon now. The idea of the two of them…" He feigns retching.

"You can move in with one of your brothers. Problem solved."

Why is this my problem? Why does everyone think they can dump their problems on me for me to solve?

"Please, pixie, don't kick me out. I don't want to live with my brothers."

I glare at him. "Do *not* call me pixie."

"Soleil, please don't make me leave," he begs.

I open my mouth to tell him it's fine, he can stay. But snap it shut when I realize I'm doing it again. I'm shouldering everyone else's problems. I steel my back. This is not my problem to solve.

"Why can't you stay with one of your brothers?"

"None of them have a spare bedroom for me."

I wave an arm toward the destroyed bed. "I don't have a spare bedroom for you now either."

He clears his throat. "But you don't treat me like a child. My brothers make fun of me and bully me about how I'm a baby. You don't."

Is he serious?

"They're teasing you. It's what siblings do."

I assume. I don't have any siblings but I've watched Ashlyn with her four sisters. They're constantly kidding and joking with each other.

He crosses his arms over his chest and I notice his t-shirt is singed. Crap. Here I am being a bitch and kicking him out and he's hurt.

"Did you burn yourself? Where are you hurt?"

I start to lift up his shirt to search for injuries but he bats me away.

"I'm fine. I'm not hurt." He smirks. "I am touched by your concern, though."

I roll my eyes. "Don't flatter yourself. I'd be concerned if a stranger was injured."

"But you wouldn't try to rip a stranger's clothes off of him."

"I wasn't ripping your clothes off of you. I was searching for injuries. There's a difference."

"All I heard was I can't wait to see your naked chest."

I throw my arms in the air. "Oh my god. You are delusional. You're hearing voices now?"

"I hear the sweet voice of my pixie girl now."

His pixie girl? I am not *his*. I'm also not a girl or a pixie.

"It's confirmed. You're delusional." I whirl around. "I'm exhausted. I'm going to bed."

"Does this mean I can stay?"

He almost sounds as if he's begging. I feel a crack in my wall of resistance. This is not good. "You can stay here tonight. We'll discuss this more in the morning."

There. I didn't totally cave the way I usually do. I mentally pat myself on the back as I turn toward the door.

"Great. I'll be there in a minute."

I freeze. "Be where in a minute?"

"In your bed of course."

I spin around to confront him. He's lucky he's not wearing a dopey grin or smirk or I'd kick him out of my house right this minute.

"Why my bed?"

He bats his eyelashes. "Where else am I going to sleep?"

"On the couch."

"You have one of those fancy couches. It's four feet long at most. I'm six-foot-one. I can't sleep on a mini couch."

I scowl at him. "I'll have you know my couch is designer."

"And really short. Too short for someone of my length to sleep on."

Damn it. He had to remind me of those long legs of his. His long torso with all of those delicious ab muscles. I clear my throat. Brody's body is not the issue here.

"You can sleep on the floor."

He gasps. "Sleep on the floor? Do you not love me anymore? Do you hate me?"

I sigh. "It's not my fault you don't have a bed to sleep in."

He approaches me and doesn't stop until he's in my space. Until I can feel his heat surrounding me. Until I can smell his sandalwood scent. I fist my hands to stop myself from reaching for him. From finally discovering how his skin feels.

"I know I screwed up. Don't worry. I'll buy you another bed."

"If you can afford a bed, why are you mooching off of me instead of living in your own apartment?"

"Have you tried to find a place to live in Winter Falls? There's nothing currently available. And I don't want to live in White Bridge. I want to live here where my family is."

Damnit. He had to say the f-word. The one word guaranteed to make my heart melt.

He reaches forward and tucks a strand of hair behind my ear. "Please don't separate me from my family."

My fists tremble as I lock my muscles down to stop myself from leaning into his hand. From closing my eyes and falling into him. I can't. He's immature and childish. Another person I would have to look after. The broken, smoldering bed is more than enough proof of his lack of maturity.

I step back and his hand falls. "Fine. You can sleep in my bed tonight."

He grins and I wag my finger at him.

"But there will be no touching. You'll stick to your side of the bed."

He salutes. "Aye! Aye! Captain!"

I start for my bedroom but stop when I remember one more thing. "And you'll wear pajamas. Bottoms and tops."

Because someone has the inclination to prowl around shirtless in the house. Not in my bed. I will not allow him to tempt me. Nope. I will resist him. I must.

Chapter 10

BRODY

My eyes fly open as I wake. I've never been one to linger in bed once I'm awake. But I pause when I feel the warmth at my back, the arm wrapped around my waist, and smell the scent of honey. *Soleil.*

I'm in her bed and she's wrapped around me. I have no idea how this happened since she insisted on making a pillow wall between the two of us before we went to sleep last night. But I am not complaining.

Quite the contrary. I capture her hand and thread my fingers through hers. Her hand tightens on mine and I smile. I know Soleil wants me. What I don't know is what's holding her back. She blames my age, but I know there's more to it.

I'm determined to figure it out. In the meantime, I'll show her I'm not an immature child. I'm a man she can rely on. Except for the whole bed incident. I know better than to fool around with fireworks inside, but I didn't want to make noise outside and disturb Soleil when she was at her pottery wheel.

Soleil moans and her free hand wanders around my hip toward my hard length. I freeze. Do I stop her? She must be asleep. She wouldn't be touching me if she were awake. She'll be mortified when she wakes up. Or do I let her touch me? Show her how I can take care of her in a very adult manner.

While I contemplate what to do, her hand reaches my cock and she squeezes. I can't help the groan from escaping.

Soleil's entire body stiffens. Shit. The fallout is not going to be pretty.

I grasp her hand and roll around until I'm facing her. She yanks on my hold.

"Let me go."

"No."

She glares at me, but her glare can't hide the heat in her eyes. I bet her nipples are hard and begging for my touch. But I'm not looking. I'm a gentleman. At least, I will be until she gives me the green light.

"You can't hold me against my will."

"I'm not holding you against your will." She tugs on her hand and I strengthen my grip. "I'm stopping you from running away before we discuss what happened."

"What is there to discuss? I was asleep. I didn't realize it was you."

"Didn't realize it was me? What did you think? I was a life-sized doll? Those things are massively expensive."

"How do you know how expensive a life-sized doll is? Never mind. Don't answer. I made a mistake. End of story."

"End of story? You crawled over the Soleil Wall to get to me. This isn't the end. This is the beginning."

"This is the beginning of nothing," she hisses. "I was asleep. You can't hold me accountable for my actions while I'm sleeping."

"What you're saying is your subconscious wants me but your conscious doesn't?"

"Exactly. I don't want you."

I ignore the sting those words cause. I know she's lying. Her conscious wants me as much as her subconscious. I may know better than to look down, but I can feel how restless her legs are. I decide to let it go for now.

"Got it."

I roll to my back and stretch my arms above my head allowing my t-shirt to hike up my chest. I finish the stretch and scratch my stomach. I can feel her gaze on my body. It's practically scorching my skin. All those weights I've lifted when I'm stuck on a coding problem have finally paid off.

I get out of bed and stroll to the door as if I don't have a care in the world. "I'm going to shower."

I whip my t-shirt off before I step into the hallway. I smile at her gasp. Challenge accepted, Ms. I Don't Want You. Challenge accepted.

When I enter the kitchen fifteen minutes later, Soleil is sitting at the kitchen bar with her phone in her hand.

"You're sure? You're absolutely positively sure?"

Her gaze flicks to mine and I slow to allow her a good long look. I'm wearing a skintight t-shirt I know matches my blue eyes to perfection. The t-shirt is uncomfortably tight, but I'm willing to sacrifice in the short term to win what I want in the long term. I'd prefer to walk around shirtless but I'm worried after how we woke up Soleil's head would explode if I did.

Soleil clears her throat before speaking into the phone, "Yes. Yes. I'm still here."

I turn toward the coffee pot to hide my smirk at her reaction. I never knew chasing a woman could be this fun. Usually, I don't have time for chasing. I'm way too busy building my company. Instead, I drop a hint about my net worth and a woman can't drop her panties fast enough for me.

I don't want Soleil to be the same as those shallow women.

She drops her phone on the counter. "Ugh. I can't believe it."

"Believe it? What's wrong?"

"There are no rental apartments or houses available in all of Winter Falls. How is this possible?"

I don't say I told you so. I think it. But I don't say it.

"Maybe because it's a small town and there isn't much real estate?" I shrug.

"I thought you were joking when you said there weren't any rentals available."

"Elder's the jokester, not me."

"Right. You're the prankster who destroyed his bed last night."

I wince. It really was a mistake. But Soleil will never believe me. Not now. Maybe I should tone down the pranks.

Nope. What a silly idea. Pranks and fun are exactly what Soleil needs. She works entirely too hard.

Plus, she's always taking care of her friends. She needs someone to care for her. And I volunteered for the job. Too bad she ripped up my application form and threw it away.

"I guess you're stuck with me."

She studies me. "What about buying a house? Are you amenable to the idea?"

I'd rather build my own. I already have my eye on the plot of land. I can't buy it yet, though. There are no secrets in Winter Falls and I'm not ready for my family to learn about my business. Soon.

"I—"

"Never mind," she cuts me off. "You obviously don't have enough money for a down payment."

Those words pierce my heart and I stumble. I have to grab hold of the kitchen counter before I fall. I know my brothers think I'm worthless. I didn't realize Soleil thought the same.

She waves her hand at me. "I mean obviously. If you had the cash, you'd already have bought a house." She narrows her eyes at me. "Wouldn't you?"

I don't want to lie. "Maybe," I hedge. "If it was a nice house."

"It doesn't matter. The house for sale is way out of your price range anyway."

I know the house she means. It's not out of my price range. It's actually on the lower end of what I want to spend. But I'm not discussing money with Soleil. I want her to want me for me. Not my money.

I grin. "You really are stuck with me."

She drums her fingers on the counter. "There must be some other solution. Explain to me why you can't live with one of your brothers again."

Crap. The last thing I want to do is explain how I don't want to live with one of my brothers because I'm not ready for them to learn about my business. Elder never paid attention to my work, but I can't be certain my other brothers will be as uninterested.

A little white lie won't hurt, though. Especially if it's based on the truth.

"All of my brothers are paired up with your friends. Don't get me wrong. I'm happy for them, but the last thing I want to do is hear one of my brothers having sex."

Soleil makes a face.

"It's bad enough I walked in on Elder and Harmony making out. Their clothes were on, but they weren't staying on for long."

"Except you purposely disturbed them."

She's not wrong. But what kind of brother would I be if I didn't tease my siblings?

"I wouldn't use the word 'purposely'."

"You saw them through the front window and barged into the house anyway."

"I needed to go to the bathroom."

"And you can only go to the bathroom at Elder's house?"

"It's the only toilet I know isn't rigged with a prank."

She wags her finger at me. "Not an excuse since you're the one who rigs the toilets for pranks."

"Let's not focus on the details."

"The details such as how no one is safe going to the bathroom in Winter Falls?"

I smirk. "I can't help it if I'm a genius at what I do."

"Being a genius at toilet pranks is nothing to be proud of."

I was actually referring to my gaming software company but anytime I bring up my games she scowls in disapproval. Which is a kick in the nuts if I'm being honest.

"You do you. I'll do me. I don't make fun of how you knit vibrator covers."

"Probably because you – for reasons I do not want to begin to think about – bought every single model I sell."

I bought them to support her. Because I was fascinated by the intricacy of the work she does. Soleil is an artist. It doesn't matter if the medium is clay or yarn – she's an artist.

"I know a good product when I see it."

She rolls her eyes. "Whatever."

"It's decided? I'm staying?"

She sighs. "You need to buy a new bed. You can't be sleeping in mine."

"I have it on good authority you enjoyed sleeping with me."

"We didn't sleep together."

I cock a brow.

"We didn't sleep together sleep together," she clarifies. "We just slept."

"Exactly. We slept together."

"You're impossible."

"Thank you. I do try."

"You're lucky I don't believe in violence."

"Or what? You'd whip me?" I lower my voice. "I'll be the one doing the whipping."

Pink colors her cheeks. Well, well. Does my little pixie enjoy getting spanked? I knew she was perfect for me.

"There will be no whipping, no tying up, no sex. Nothing of the sort."

I can't help myself from adding, "But we will be sleeping together."

"Platonically. With clothes on. And a barrier between us."

A barrier didn't stop her from crawling to me last night.

"If I agree to the above conditions, may I continue to live with you?"

"You can stay here until you find somewhere else to live. And I want you actively searching for some place to stay. No more of this letting things happen. Plus, you need to buy a new bed to replace the one you broke."

"Done." I reach out my hand. When her hand touches mine, I lift it to my lips. "Thank you," I say before brushing a kiss over her knuckles.

A pulse flutters in her neck. "You're welcome." When her voice comes out all breathy, she clears her throat. "Now get to ordering a bed."

She pulls her hand away and jumps off the kitchen stool before marching away.

You can run as far and as fast as you want, pixie girl. I'm going to catch you anyway.

Chapter 11

I CREEP DOWN THE hallway to my bedroom. I don't want to wake Brody. Waking Brody means dealing with him sleeping in my bed next to me a mere arm's length away. My body warms at the idea. Stupid body. Yearning after someone I can't have.

I thought last night was a one-and-done. I was convinced I'd be able to find him somewhere else to live today. Even after I agreed he could stay at my house, I continued to phone and send messages to everyone in town who I know has a spare bedroom.

No one has space for him. Apparently, everyone in Winter Falls has decided to turn their spare room into an office or a gym or a movie room. I guess no one expects any family to visit.

I even reached out to Ashlyn's sister Ellery, the owner of the *Inn on Main,* the bed and breakfast in town. When I asked if she had any openings, she literally burst into laughter. I wasn't joking.

I inhale a deep breath before opening my bedroom door. I frown at the sight in front of me. Brody is sitting up in bed with his computer in his lap.

"Made yourself comfortable, haven't you?"

He shuts the laptop. "I was waiting up for you."

My brow wrinkles. "Why are you waiting up for me? We aren't a couple."

"I wanted to make sure you got home safe before I went to sleep."

"Got home safe? I work in the backyard."

He shrugs. "I don't care."

I ignore how the idea of him waiting up for me to make sure I'm safe makes me feel all warm and fuzzy. "You really don't understand Winter Falls."

"I love this crazy, eccentric town. What's there to understand?"

"Winter Falls is the safest small town in the world."

"Unless you happen to run naked down Main Street," he mutters.

"What did you say?" I ask because he seriously didn't just say he ran down Main Street naked. I must be hearing things.

"Nothing," he mumbles.

He sets the computer on the nightstand revealing his naked chest. I glance away before I start to stare. No staring at Brody's chest no matter how delicious it appears.

"You're breaking the rules. We agreed – you have to wear pajama tops and bottoms."

"It's ninety degrees out and you don't have air conditioning."

I gasp. "Air conditioning? I wouldn't dare."

Air conditioning is horrible for the environment. You need special dispensation to have an air conditioner in Winter Falls.

Thus far, the only businesses granted an exception are the yoga studio and the restaurants. No single family residence has air conditioning.

"Fine. I'll put on a top." He flings the sheet back and stands.

My eyes disobey my orders and peek over at him. "You're wearing boxers!"

He wiggles his ass. "Thanks for noticing."

I fix my gaze on the ceiling before the sight of his ass in those skintight boxers tempts me to do something I would never normally do. Such as touch him. Ask him to move those stupid boxers out of the way of what I want. I stuff my hands in my pockets. No touching!

"Boxers are not pajamas," I grit out.

"Do I need to remind you about the ninety degrees thing again?"

"I don't need a reminder. I spent the day in my pottery shed with the kiln on. If you want to compare who has it the toughest, I'm winning."

"Then, you understand how uncomfortable it is for me to wear sweats to bed," he says instead of acknowledging what I said.

I snort. "Seriously? I wore a long-sleeved t-shirt and jeans all day long. You'll get no sympathy from me."

"But my sweats are too warm," he complains.

"Don't you have any pajama bottoms?"

"I don't usually wear pajamas. In fact," he lowers his voice to a gentle rumble that does not make my knees knock. It doesn't! "I usually sleep in the nude."

Stupid knees are definitely knocking now. "You are not sleeping in the nude with me," I say to draw attention away from my unstable knees.

"Thus, the boxers."

"Go find something else to wear. For all I care, wear a pair of jeans. It doesn't matter. But your legs will be appropriately covered."

"Geez. I didn't know you were such a prude. Aren't Winter Falls natives supposed to be all laissez-faire about sex?"

He had to say the s-word, didn't he? Great. Now I can't stop imagining him naked above me and plunging into me.

I mentally slap myself upside the head. *Enough, Soleil.* Roommates. You are roommates. Nothing more.

"I'm showering," I say as I stomp toward the bathroom. "If you want to sleep in a bed tonight, put on some pants."

I slam the door behind me before collapsing against it. How am I going to survive sleeping in the same bed with Brody and not attacking him? He better have paid extra for expedited delivery when he bought the replacement bed.

Chapter 12

Has anyone in this town heard of the word privacy? ~ Message from Brody on the Winter Falls Facebook page

I ENTER THE COURTHOUSE building where the Winter Falls monthly business meetings are held and peek inside the meeting room to scan for Brody. Phew. He's in the back with his brothers while my friends are sitting near the front of the room.

Good. I can avoid him.

It seems silly to avoid a man who's staying in my house but I can't chance the rest of Winter Falls finding out about how attracted I am to him. Everyone will jump on the bandwagon to push us together. Never mind how *I* don't want to be attracted to Brody.

I creep to where my friends are sitting while keeping one eye out for Brody.

"Why are you sneaking around?" Ashlyn asks loud enough for the people in White Bridge, a thirty-minute drive away, to hear.

"I'm not sneaking around," I lie.

She barks out a laugh. "And I'm not horny."

"You're always horny," Moon says.

Ashlyn smiles. "Exactly."

"How does your husband keep up with you?" I ask.

Her smile becomes wicked. "Don't you worry. Rowan has plenty of stamina. I'd recommend dating a former football player, but I think you've got your eye on a different man."

I scowl. "I don't have my eye on any man."

Eden chuckles. "You heard it here first, folks. We're still in the denial phase."

I narrow my eyes at her. "I'm not in denial."

Harmony elbows me. "There's no sense fighting it. Love will win in the end."

"Where's Robin? I want my cuddles." If I have to put up with my friends teasing me, I deserve a reward. And what better reward is there than cuddles from a baby?

Harmony points to the back of the room where Elder is holding their baby with the rest of his brothers gathered around him. Brody catches my gaze and waves. I ignore him and whirl around in my seat.

"Whoa. Slow down." Eden grasps my shoulder before I fall off the chair. She's exaggerating. I'm a teensy weensy bit wobbly. Nothing more.

"What is Brody doing here anyway?" I mutter. "He doesn't own a business."

"I don't?"

Crap. How is Brody standing right behind me? Did he sprint across the room?

"Why are sneaking up on me?" I snap at him.

"I wasn't sneaking but if you want me to be sneaky, I can be." He waggles his eyebrows.

The last thing I need is for Brody to be sneaky. I need for him to stay firmly on the outside of the walls I've erected around my heart, especially for him. I put signs up and everything. *Brody stay out!*

I put on a sigh. "Always acting the child."

Pain flashes in his eyes. Damnit. I'm a bitch. I swear I'm usually a nice person. But when Brody's around 'normal' Soleil takes a hike.

I search for a change of subject as the rest of the Bragg brothers join us.

"Don't you need to get this meeting started?" I ask Moon as she's currently the acting mayor.

"I'll be glad when this gig is over," she grumbles as she gets to her feet.

"Ha!" Eden snorts. "Now you understand why I didn't want to be mayor."

Moon rolls her eyes. "You didn't want to be mayor because you were having your whole foreplay spat with Miller."

Eden shrugs. "It worked out in the end."

She makes it sound as if her argument with Miller was no big deal. She wishes. Miller and Eden staged verbal combat against each other for more than a year. The argument was supposedly about how the expansion of Miller's brewery would ruin the gardens behind her plant shop, *Eden's Gardens.*

But really, they just wanted each other and were fighting it because of stupid reasons. They finally managed to get over their issues. They're now blissfully happy together and apparently trying for a baby. Another thing I refuse to be jealous of.

Moon walks to the front of the room to oversee the meeting and the Bragg brothers sit behind us.

Ashlyn hands me a beer. "Here. Today's word is bed."

I purse my lips. "A business meeting is not the place for a drinking game."

"And yet. Here we are."

There's no arguing with the crazy woman. I accept the beer, but I won't be playing her game. I never do. Someone has to be the adult in this friendship.

"I now call the July business meeting for Winter Falls to order." Moon bangs her gavel on the table. "The first item on the agenda is the Lammas festival."

Ashlyn's sister, Lilac, stands next to Moon. She's the comptroller for Winter Falls despite no longer living in town since she met and married the man of her dreams.

I sigh. Why is everyone finding the man of their dreams and I'm not? At thirty-eight, I'm the oldest of the single ladies. I should be married with a couple of kids already.

A hand squeezes my shoulder. "Are you okay?" Brody whispers in my ear.

I inhale a deep breath to center myself to stop the full body shiver threatening to occur at the feel of his breath against my neck.

"I believe we should discuss the profit for the Litha festival first," Lilac says.

"You have everything under control," Sage shouts from the rear of the room.

"Thank—"

"There's no need to discuss the profit," Sage interrupts. "I want to discuss *that*."

What's she talking about? I glance around the room but everyone is staring at me.

"What's going on?" I ask.

"Someone's got the gossip gals' attention," Ashlyn sings.

"Stupid Project Cub," I mutter. I was hoping the gossip gals would forget about us. I should be so lucky.

"What's going on?" Mrs. Bragg asks.

Oh great. I feel my face warm. We're doing this in front of Brody's mom? Awesome. This is exactly how I want to meet the mom of the person I'm living with. Whoa! Hold the phone! I'm not living with Brody. He's staying in my house because he has nowhere else to live. Nothing more.

Except we're sharing a bed. But not because I want to! Shit. I'm lying to myself. I don't want to want to share a bed with Brody. There. Those words aren't a lie.

"Rumor has it your son and Soleil have been sleeping in the same bed," Cayenne says.

"Drink!" Ashlyn shouts and I snap my teeth at her.

Petal sighs. "Project Cub is my favorite."

"I'm glad my book recommendation worked out for you," Feather adds.

I jump to my feet. "We're not sleeping together."

"Why not? You're gorgeous. My son has a crush on you. Go for it," Mrs. Bragg says.

"Mrs. Bragg," I begin.

"It's Daisy."

"Daisy, your son and I aren't together."

"But you slept in the same bed last night," Clove claims.

"Drink!" I pinch Ashlyn this time since snapping my teeth at her has no effect. Honestly, nothing I do will probably deter her, but I'm not giving up.

I narrow my eyes on Clove. "How do you know Brody and I slept in the same…" I clear my throat before I use the word bed. "How do you know where Brody slept last night?"

Peace growls as he gets to his feet. "I told you if I caught you peeking in any windows again, I'd confiscate your binoculars."

Sage bats her eyelashes at him. "But you didn't catch us."

He crosses his arms over his chest. "How else do you know they slept in the same bed?"

"Dri—" Ashlyn's husband slams a hand over her mouth before she can finish speaking. I nod to him in thanks.

Sage snorts. "Because Soleil only has one bed currently in her house."

"And you know this how?"

"Why else would Brody order a new bed?" Cayenne asks.

"Unless they started the other bed on fire," Petal answers. "You should really let the fire department put out fires. They're the experts. Plus, the firemen are pretty to look at."

I moan and bury my face in my hands.

Brody stands and wraps an arm around me. "I appreciate everyone's concern over how many be— places to sleep Soleil has in her house, but our relationship is no one's business but ours."

Laughter erupts.

"Did you hear?"

"He thinks privacy exists in Winter Falls."

"It's cute."

"He'll learn."

"It's not as if he's going anywhere."

"Not when Soleil is here to stay."

"AHEM!" Brody clears his throat with such force I'm afraid he may have hurt his vocal cords. "I don't care if Winter Falls doesn't believe in privacy. I don't care how small towns work. The only thing I care about is protecting Soleil's privacy."

I squash the butterflies threatening to awaken at his words. This is no time for butterflies. Besides, they're not allowed out when it comes to Brody.

"You made things ten times worse."

He squeezes my middle. "Don't worry. I'll handle everyone." He glances around at the people staring at us. "At the very least, I'll install shutters on your house."

He'll handle everything? He can't possibly know how I long for a man to handle everything. How much I wish someone would take care of me for once instead of the other way around.

Knock it off, Soleil. Brody is not the man for you. He's an immature prankster, remember?

Chapter 13

I GROAN WHEN THE phone rings and wakes me in the middle of
the night.

"Make it stop," I mutter as I cuddle into my pillow.

My warm, life-sized pillow. Wait a minute. I don't have a
life-sized pillow. I draw my hand along the pillow and encounter
smooth skin. I yank my hand away. Nope. This is not a pillow.

I knife up in bed. "What the hell? Why are you on my side
of the bed?" I yell at Brody.

Brody yawns before nodding to the other side of the bed –
my side of the bed – which is completely and totally empty
since I'm practically laying on top of him on his side. How did
I get here?

"I don't get it," I say as I look back and forth between the sides
of the bed. "Where's the Soleil Wall?"

"Where it is every night until I put it back together before
you wake up." He nods toward the floor where all the pillows
are piled up.

"You reassemble the wall every morning?"

"And put a shirt on," he says as he grabs his t-shirt from the floor.

This makes zero sense. How did this happen?

"I don't get it. Am I dreaming?"

He grins. "I've been living my dream every night for the past two weeks."

I slap his shoulder. "I'm being serious here."

He captures my hand. "Me too."

"This is a disaster." I tug on my hand but he refuses to let me go.

"Why is it a disaster? Nothing untoward has happened beyond a bit of innocent cuddling."

I frown. Sleeping in one bed is obviously not working. How could I not know I'm cuddling Brody in my sleep every night? I wake up on my side in the morning. Dream Soleil is apparently a hussy. She needs to be stopped.

"Maybe I should sleep on the couch until the new bed arrives."

Spoiler alert – I don't want to sleep on the couch. I want to cuddle Brody every night. And not only when I'm sleeping and can't remember how it feels to be wrapped together all night long.

Knock it off, Soleil. There will be no cuddling with Brody for you.
Brody snorts. "Even you aren't short enough to fit on your couch."

"I'm being serious."

He scowls. "So am I. There's no way I'm letting you sleep on a couch, which is way too short for you."

"Letting me?" I snarl. "Who the hell do you think you are?"

"Whoa." He holds up his palms. "I was referring to how hard you work and how your job is physically demanding. You need to sleep in a bed."

Hold the phone. He knows my job is physically demanding? All my friends think I sit around on my ass all day. I may be sitting but my core muscles and arms are stabilizing the clay while my hands shape it and my foot controls the speed of the wheel.

I narrow my eyes on him. "How do you know my job is physically demanding?"

He bites his lips and glances away. "I might have done some research on making pottery."

"You did…" I trail off. Now is not the time to question Brody's Google searches. Or think he's super sweet for studying my craft. Nope. Not now. There are more important things to discuss here.

"We can't continue this way."

He scowls. "Why not? There's nothing to stress about. We've done a little cuddling. Nothing more."

I raise my eyebrows. "Nothing more but yet you were topless."

His cheeks darken. "You got annoyed if I wore a top."

I what? Oh. My. God. Kill me now. Please tell me this is a dream. *Please be sleeping.* I pinch myself and yelp. Ouch. Damn. I'm awake. I bury my face in my hands.

"Please tell me I didn't fondle you in my sleep."

He grasps my wrists and pulls my hands away from my face. "You didn't fondle me in my sleep." He wiggles his eyebrows. "Although any fondling from you would have been enjoyed."

"Can you be serious for one minute?"

"I am being serious. Nothing happened I didn't want to happen."

"Maybe I didn't want it to happen," I pout.

"Your sleep cuddling says otherwise."

I cough to hide my laugh. "Sleep cuddling? I don't think sleep cuddling is a real thing."

"I have two weeks of proof it is."

He rubs his thumbs against the skin of my inner wrists and my whole body warms. My body isn't interested in cuddling. It wants to declare cuddling time officially over. It's now time to jump Brody and show him the ride of his life. My panties dampen as I imagine how good it would feel to be on top of him, riding him, his naked body on display for me.

"I really should sleep on the couch," I mutter as my body leans toward Brody.

His eyes focus on my lips and I bite my bottom lip. He groans before he—

My telephone rings again and Brody swears before snatching it up from the nightstand. "Always answer your phone if it rings in the middle of the night."

"Excuse me. I'm the responsible one here. Not you."

He doesn't respond as he hands me my phone.

"Hello," I answer.

"Oh, thank goodness," Harmony says. "I need your help."

At the word 'help', all thoughts of Brody and his body and the cuddling I'm allegedly doing at night fly out of my mind. I roll out of bed. "Of course. I'm on my way."

She giggles. "Don't you want to know what help I need first?"

"Not unless you need me to bring a shovel to bury a body."

"If she needs help burying Elder, I'll bring an extra shovel," Brody says.

"Do I hear Brody?" Harmony asks.

"He's a guest in my house or have you forgotten?"

"He sounds awful close." She gasps. "Holy bats of Gotham! You two *are* sleeping in the same bed. This is awesome."

"Is there an actual emergency or did you phone to get the scoop to use for your bet on Project Cub?" I growl.

"Oh, there's an emergency, *and* I will be using this information to place my bet."

"What's the emergency?" I ask because from here on out I'm pretending the bet doesn't exist. Project Cub? What's that? Never heard of it.

"I'm having problems with a very naughty llama."

I giggle "Lucy never learns her lesson, does she?"

"I wish," she mutters. "She escaped the refuge. Again. Maybe we should set her free. She deserves her freedom. But she's used to being fed several times a day. I don't know if she'd make it on her own. Besides, llamas aren't native to North America, and she—"

"Maybe we should discuss finding Lucy now and you can have an existential crisis about whether animals should be in cages later."

She blows out a breath. "You're right. Can you search the area south of the refuge? I'm heading north."

"Got it," I say and hang up.

I hurry toward my dresser to dig out some clothes but stop when I notice Brody snatch a pair of sweatpants from the floor.

"What are you doing?"

"Duh. Coming with you."

"But you don't even know where I'm going or what I'm doing."

He shrugs. "Doesn't matter. I know you're going out in the middle of the night to help a friend. I don't need to know more."

"Lucy the llama escaped the refuge again," I explain.

"That llama is a menace," he grumbles as he marches toward the hallway with his clothes in his hands. When I stand there staring at him like a ninny, he stops and glances over his shoulder at me. "What's wrong?"

"You're coming to help?"

He rolls his eyes. "Of course, I am."

Why would he help? It makes no sense. Except Harmony and Elder are married. He's not helping me. He's helping his brother. Now, it makes sense.

"I guess all of the Bragg brothers will probably come to help."

"I don't give a shit about my brothers. I care about you. I'm not letting you go out in the middle of the night all alone."

"But this is Winter Falls. It's perfectly safe." I'm beginning to sound like a broken record.

"I wouldn't care if you had a team of bodyguards with you. You aren't going out in the middle of the night on your own."

At his words, a crack forms in the wall around my heart designed to keep him out. If I'm being totally honest with myself – something I prefer not to do when it comes to Brody Bragg – there are already several cracks in the wall. I don't know how long I can keep this wall erect.

Or how long *I want* to keep this wall erect.

Lucy's not the only one in trouble.

Chapter 14

Is Xanax a prescription drug? Or can I pick some up at the drugstore? ~ Text from Brody to the Bragg brothers

BRODY

"What the hell are you doing?" Soleil asks.

I groan and roll to my back. "What do I appear to be doing?"

She scans the spare bedroom. There isn't much to see. I got rid of any remnants of the bed.

"Building a blanket fort?"

A blanket fort sounds fun. Gathering every extra blanket in the house to build a mattress to cushion sleeping on the floor is not.

"Why are you sleeping on the floor?"

"What other option do I have?" I get to my feet and stretch my back. "You don't want me sleeping with you."

And there was no way I'd continue sleeping in her bed when it makes her uncomfortable. She should be comfortable in her own home.

She motions toward the blankets. "I didn't expect you to sleep on the floor."

"I'm not sleeping on your miniature couch."

She scowls. "I told you. My couch is designer. It's not minia-ture."

I'm not having this argument again.

"What do you need?" I ask instead.

Her eyes flare with heat for a moment and I silently beg her to admit what we both know – she wants me. She clears her throat and the flames die. I sigh.

"I… um… woke up and you weren't there and I got worried something happened to you."

I scratch my stomach – my bare stomach – and she licks her lips. "I'm perfectly fine."

Her gaze stops on the clock on the dresser. "Shit. I need to hurry. Today is Lammas." She rushes away.

I quickly dress while Soleil showers. By the time she's dressed, I have breakfast ready for her.

"Good morning," I greet when she flies into the kitchen.

"No time. Busy day. Need to get going."

I hand her a mug of coffee. "Here you go."

She downs half the mug in one go. As usual. I've learned to melt an ice cube in her coffee. I'm not having her burn her esophagus. I don't care if she says the heat doesn't bother her. I'm not chancing it.

"Exactly what I needed."

"You're welcome."

She rolls her eyes. "Thank you for the coffee, Brody."

I hand her a plate of eggs and bacon.

"I don't have time to eat."

I nudge her toward the table. "We have time. The pottery is already loaded in the truck."

Her mouth gapes open. "The pottery is already loaded in the truck?"

"You heard me. I loaded the pottery last night." I nudge her toward a bar stool. "Sit. Eat. You need your strength for today."

She digs into her food. "Done. Done. Still to do," she mutters as she scrolls through the to-do lists on her phone.

I snatch her phone from her.

"Give it back."

I shove it in my back pocket. "No. After you finish eating your breakfast you can have your phone."

"You're not my dad."

"Damn straight I'm not." My feelings for Soleil are not paternal. "Eat."

"You're supposed to be a dork. Not bossy."

I grin. "Don't worry. I can be both."

I watch as she inhales the food off the plate. I debate giving her seconds but she holds out her hand and wiggles her fingers at me. "Phone. Now. Don't make me hurt you."

"I'd love to see you try," I mumble as I place the phone in her hand.

While she reviews her lists for the day, I put away her plate and fill a to-go mug with coffee for her.

"Ready?" I ask as I hand her the mug.

She narrows her eyes at me. "Why are you being nice to me?"

I lock my body before I flinch at her question. I'm always nice to her. I make her coffee every morning. I also have breakfast ready for her most mornings. I mow the lawn. I even cleaned out the gutters.

The only thing I don't do for her is clean the inside of the house. I would. Despite what my brother Elder thinks, I'm not opposed to cleaning. But the first – and last – time I cleaned, she complained my vacuuming was not up to snuff. Apparently, you need to leave lines in the carpet.

"I'm always nice." Especially to her.

She snorts. "And you didn't prank me by dressing up as a ghost either."

I'll never admit this out loud but dressing up as a ghost to scare Soleil in order to 'save' her from said ghost wasn't my best idea ever. Don't tell my brothers. I'd never hear the end of it.

"I can be nice *and* pull a prank."

"Really? How is putting googly eyes on all the items in the fridge nice?"

"I didn't say all my pranks are nice."

"That's for damn sure. There's nothing nice about dressing up a goat like a princess."

"How do you know about the goat?"

"Or removing a battery from a police vehicle."

"Hey, now. There's no proof it was me." She lifts her eyebrows and stares at me. Fuck. I can't lie to this woman. "Shouldn't we get going?"

She checks the oven clock. "Shit. We're late."

She dashes for the door, but I catch her hand. "Slow down. We're not late."

"Easy for you to say. You don't know the pressure of running a business and depending on a single weekend to bring in a significant portion of your revenue."

I don't? If my company doesn't do well at Christmas, my balance sheet cries red ink. I don't tell Soleil about my business, though. Someday I will. But not today when she's in total stress out mode.

I lace my fingers through hers. "Let's go."

She blows out a breath. "Okay. I got this."

We arrive at the community center less than five minutes later. Another ten minutes and all the pottery crates are unloaded.

"I'll unbox the pottery and you can set it up however you want," I say as I open the first crate with a crowbar.

"You can go. My friends will help me."

I cock an eyebrow. "They will?"

"Moon can help."

"She's busy running the diner all day."

Most of Soleil's friends also depend on the influx of revenue from the festival weekends. Thanks to Riley, I know Moon, in particular, is anxious about making enough cash at her diner from this weekend.

"Eden then."

"She's got her shop to run."

"Harmony! Harmony will help."

I cough to hide my smile. Harmony would help, but she's been given quite the incentive to claim baby Robin is sick. Incentive as in a nice wad of cash. Cash she promises she won't tell Elder or my other brothers about.

"You can phone her while I unload the pottery."

"Be careful," she orders before fishing out her phone and walking away.

In less than a minute, she returns with a scowl on her face.

"What's wrong?" I ask.

"Baby Robin's sick." She bites her lip. "Maybe I should go check on her and Harmony since Elder's working at the brewery all day."

The struggle of what to do is clearly visible on her face as she glances around at the pottery I've laid out. Fuck. I didn't mean for her to worry. I just wanted her to need me for once. The way I need her.

I approach and grasp her hands. "There's no need for you to check on the baby."

Her brow wrinkles. "I don't know. Robin's barely a few months old. Harmony would be devastated if something happened to her."

Damnit. I'm the world's biggest asshole. Robin is Harmony's only living relative. And Harmony would be beyond devastated if Robin became seriously ill. But she's not ill at all. No, Harmony's lying on my behalf.

"There's no reason to worry."

"How do you know?"

Crap. I need to come clean. This is not going to go well for me.

"I know because I asked Harmony to lie for me and say the baby's sick."

Soleil yanks out of my hold. "You did what? You had me worried for nothing!"

"I'm sorry. I wanted to be the one to help you out today."

Her nose scrunches in confusion. "You asked my friend to lie to me so you could help out today?"

I don't know if she's asking but I nod just in case.

She slaps my shoulder. "How dare you? I was sick with worry! Nothing can happen to Robin. I won't let it. Not after everything Harmony has gone through. I won't let my friend suffer alone. She is going to get her happily ever after. I don't care what I have to do to make it happen."

"You!" She stabs me with her finger. "You lied to me. How dare you lie to me? How childish are you? Lying to get your way. You are—"

"You give me no choice," I mutter before I slam my mouth down on hers.

Her taste of honey is intoxicating. I want more. I bite her bottom lip and she gasps, allowing me to press my tongue into her mouth. She clutches my shoulders to bring me closer.

Don't worry, Soleil. I'll come as close as you want. In fact. I grasp her hip and lift her leg up until she wraps it around my waist opening herself to me. I punch my hips and my hard length hits her belly.

She moans as her fingernails dig into her shoulders. *Dig as hard as you want, pixie girl. Mark me. Make me yours.*

"Well. Well. Well. What do we have here?"

At the sound of Harmony's voice, I slow the kiss before pulling away from Soleil.

"This was a mistake," she mutters before running away.

Damn it. I rub a hand down my face. I finally had Soleil right where I want her and she thinks it was a mistake. Guess I'll have to show her it wasn't.

Chapter 15

"I can't believe you. How dare you?" I hiss at Harmony.

She bats her eyelashes and clasps her chest. "How dare I? I'm not the one who helped my husband plan a surprise wedding without warning me."

I snort. "Don't lie to me. You freaking loved the wedding."

Her eyes lose focus and her face gets all dreamy as her gaze lands on Elder standing across the room with his brothers. "Yeah."

Damn. I want what she has. A husband who loves me. Who would go all out to plan the perfect wedding for me as a surprise. Never mind Harmony and Elder were already married. The first wedding ceremony was fake. This one definitely was not.

Despite the surprise, Harmony didn't waste any time at the reception in seating me next to Brody. She's also claiming we're part of the wedding 'party' and have to dance together. Thus, me hissing at her.

"Stop playing matchmaker and go enjoy your evening with your husband," I push.

She barks out a laugh. She laughs and laughs and laughs. I cross my arms over my chest and glare at her. I don't think this situation is funny at all.

"What's so funny?" Eden asks as she sits down next to me.

"Nothing," I grumble.

"It must be something," Moon says as she joins us.

"What are we talking about?" Ashlyn asks as she plops down on a chair. "I'm guessing Brody and Soleil."

"There is no Brody and Soleil."

And there never will be. Nope. I've reinforced my walls against the man. And since he's not sleeping in the same bed as me anymore, I can keep him at arm's length.

Yeah, right. Because living in the same house as him isn't tempting in and of itself. And then there's the kiss we shared. The panty-melting kiss.

Harmony snorts. "Sure there isn't."

Ashlyn hones in on her. "What do you know?"

Harmony bites her lip. "Nothing."

Ashlyn narrows her eyes on Harmony. "Are you keeping information to yourself in order to win the Project Cub bet? Not cool, lady. Not cool."

Stupid gossip gals thinking they're matchmakers and setting up betting pools. See if I ever give them a discount to attend one of my pottery classes again.

Eden leans forward. "I don't care about the bet. I want Harmony to spill the beans."

"Me too." Moon grins. "Do I need to order a Bragg woman t-shirt?"

Ashlyn chuckles. "Because you didn't already order one for Soleil."

I glare at Moon. "You better not have ordered me a Bragg woman t-shirt."

"Okay." She shrugs. "We'll pretend I didn't."

Eden studies me. "She's not trying to stop the Ashlyn and Moon show. She always tries to stop those two from bickering unless…" Her eyes widen. "What happened?"

I sniff and lift my nose in the air. "I don't know what you're referring to."

She shoves her palm in my face. "I'm not talking to you. I want to hear from Harmony what happened."

"Harmony," I growl. She better not tattle to our friends.

"It's for your own good," she tells me before turning toward Eden, Moon, and Ashlyn. "Brody and Soleil were kissing at the Lammas festival. And not a mere peck on the lips. No, they were *going at it*. If I hadn't walked in on them, clothes would have gone flying."

Ashlyn slaps her hand down on the table. "I knew it!"

"It doesn't mean anything," I claim.

"Which is why Brody's been undressing you with his eyes all night." Eden waves at Brody across the room.

I glance over and as soon as Brody catches me looking, he begins prowling across the room. The first chords of *Lover* from Taylor Swift begin to play and I roll my eyes. Brody thinks I'm a Swiftie. I mean. I am. But he shouldn't know what music I prefer to listen to.

He stops in front of me and holds out his hand before bowing. "May I have this dance, milady?"

I don't get a chance to tell him *hell no* before Ashlyn is pushing me out of my chair. "Go," she hisses.

Brody doesn't hesitate. He catches my hand as I'm forced to my feet and draws me near before kissing my cheek.

"They're so cute together," Harmony squeals and I flip her off behind my back.

"Classy. Such a classy lady," Love Hill snarks.

Love Hill is Winter Falls' very own mean girl. She thinks it's a sport to steal men from their partners. She probably has a scoreboard somewhere in her dungeon where she keeps track of how many hearts she's broken.

"Damon!" Brody shouts before pointing at Love Hill. "Deal with it."

Brody's oldest brother, who's visiting for the wedding, sighs before marching toward Love Hill. Her gaze rakes over him before she licks her lips.

"You should go help your brother. Love Hill will devour him without a second thought."

Brody chuckles. "Damon can handle her. Besides, I believe you owe me a dance." He spins me until I end up plastered to him. "There. Much better."

I push him away to create some space between us. "Much better for whom? My girlfriends are going to tease me about this dance until the end of days."

He tweaks my nose. "Sounds fair since my brothers have spent the entire evening bawking at me for being a chicken for not asking you to dance."

My brow wrinkles. "But the music just started."

"Ah, facts have no effect on teasing amongst brothers."

"I wouldn't know."

He draws me near once again. "Did you want siblings when you were growing up?"

"I did but it wouldn't have been fair."

"Wouldn't have been fair? What do you mean?"

Shit. Why did I open my big mouth?

"Nothing. Forget what I said."

I can feel his body quake with his laughter. "You're cute thinking I'll forget anything you say. I remember every single word you've ever spoken to me."

"Stalker much?"

"I have a deal for you."

I tilt my head back to look up at him. "You have a deal for me? What's this deal? What bargaining chips do you have? Or did you forget you're mooching off me for a place to live?"

Hurt flashes in his eyes. Damn it. I'm a bitch. I promise I'm not normally a bitch but when Brody's around my hormones go into overload and I blurt things out I shouldn't. All in an attempt to keep him at arm's length. I glance down at how our bodies are touching from shoulder to hip.

Great job, Soleil. Keep it up. At this pace, you'll probably sleep with him before the night is over.

Sleep with him? Visions of him in my bed pop into my mind. But he's not wearing clothes the way he did before. No, in these visions, he's completely and utterly naked. I bite my lip as I imagine getting my hands on all of his muscles.

His eyes heat as he stares down at me. "Whatever you're thinking at this moment, I'm down with."

"Maybe I'm imagining covering your body in honey and abandoning you in the yard near my beehives."

"Kinky."

I giggle. Leave it to Brody to respond to a threat with 'kinky'. "You're crazy."

He grins. "And proud of it."

Ashlyn crashes into me, and I push her away. "What are you doing?"

"Sorry. I got carried away dancing."

Carried away dancing? This is a slow song. Why is she jumping around like she's in desperate need of the bathroom?

I glance around and notice the dance floor is packed with people jumping around. Hold on. This isn't a slow song. When did the song end?

"I'm going to win this bet," Sage declares as she does the twist next to me.

"Don't bet on it!" Cayenne shouts back at her.

"Project Cub is my favorite!" Petal yells.

I groan and shove my face into Brody's chest. "Great. Freaking great."

Brody sways me from side to side as if the slow song was still playing. "I think it's more than great."

I glance up at him. "You're such a dork."

"I'm *your* dork."

I scowl at him. "You're not my anything."

He smirks. "You're cuddled in my arms swaying to the music while everyone else is dancing the twist. I'm winning."

Why am I still cuddled in his arms? Why aren't I pushing him away? I don't want him. My body calls me a liar. Okay. Fine. I don't want to want him. There. Are you happy? My body would be much happier if I lost all of my clothes and went horizontal with Brody.

Not happening. I'm in charge here. Not my body.

River Alston, a kid I grew up with here in Winter Falls, plows his way onto the dance floor.

"Soleil!" he shouts.

I smile at him. "What's up, River?"

He frowns. "I need you to come with me."

Brody steps in front of me, blocking River's view of me. "What's wrong?"

"You can come, too," River says to Brody. "I'll give you a ride."

Brody grasps my hand and we follow River out of the barn at the Wildlife Refuge where Harmony's wedding reception is taking place.

"What's going on?"

River doesn't answer but points to a golf cart. "Hop in."

Before I was curious. Now, I'm downright terrified. What is happening?

Chapter 16

I CLING TO BRODY's hand as River drives us away from the Wildlife Refuge.

"Will you at least tell me where we're going?" I ask River.

"To your place."

"Why? I promise I was behaving." I try to make light of the situation but he merely grunts in return.

Brody wraps an arm around my shoulders. "Whatever it is, it'll be okay." He kisses my hair and I lean into him.

Time slows to a crawl during the ride from the refuge to my house. I'm strangling Brody's hand but he doesn't complain.

"Brace yourselves," River says as we turn the corner into my street.

Brace ourselves for what? I don't get the chance to ask the question before I see it. Smoke. Fire. The street full of emergency vehicles.

"Whoa!" Brody catches me as I try to jump out of the golf cart. "Wait until we come to a stop."

"Come to a stop?" I shriek. "My house is on fire. Who gives a flying flute about coming to a stop?"

"Not your house," River mutters as he parks.

I jump out but Brody keeps hold of my hand to stop me from running away.

River steps in front of us. "I didn't lie. It's not your house."

My shoulders drop as I blow out a breath in relief. "Not my house. Thank goodness. Whose house is it? I hope it's not my neighbor's house. Saffron can't get around very well." I gasp. "Oh no. Is Saffron okay?"

"Saffron is fine. And her house isn't on fire."

I try to peek past River, but he's more than a foot taller than me. Being short sucks sometimes. "Whose house is it? You said it wasn't my house. Were you lying?"

He drags a hand down his face. "It wasn't a house. We managed to save the house."

"Save the house. Wasn't a house? What do you— No! No! No! No!" I sprint for my house. My backyard to be precise.

It can't be. My pottery shed can't be on fire. It can't be. I can't lose my pottery shed. I can't. I round my house and come to a screeching halt. My pottery shed is no more. The only thing remaining is the blackened ground where I used to make my art.

"NO!"

I fall to my knees and Brody scoops me up. He cradles me in his arms as I whale my fists against his chest.

"This isn't fair! I've lost everything! What am I going to do?"

I burst into tears and Brody holds me close as he rocks me back and forth. He doesn't speak, merely embraces me as the tears flow down my cheeks, and I cling to him. He feels strong. As if he can protect me from the world.

When the tears slow and I'm left hiccupping, he pushes my hair out of my face and palms my neck. "River wants to talk to us. You up for it?"

"What choice do I have?" I pout.

"If you don't want to talk to him now, I'll tell him to leave. He can come back later."

I blow out a breath. This isn't me. Soleil isn't a pouter. "No. Let's get this over with."

He lifts me from his lap before standing and offering me his hand. I frown as I notice the soot and grass stains on his suit.

"I ruined your suit."

He shrugs. "No big deal. It's just clothing."

"Just clothing? Suits aren't cheap. I'll have it cleaned or buy you a new one."

His jaw clenches. "You aren't buying me a fucking suit."

"But you don't have another suit and I've ruined this one."

"You didn't ruin it. We'll discuss this later."

"But—"

He places a finger on my lips. "I know you want a distraction from what's happening, but you need to talk to River at some point."

I nod. Since when is he the adult in this relationship?

Brody places his hand on my hip and steers me toward where River is standing with the other volunteer firefighters. I forgot he's a volunteer firefighter when he came to pick us up, which is probably for the better. I would have lost my mind on the ride home convinced the home my mother left me was gone.

River steps away from the group and joins us in the middle of my lawn.

"What happened?" Brody asks.

River scratches his beard. "It's too soon to know for certain, but it appears to be an electrical fire."

My heart stalls in my chest. There's only one main source of electricity in my shed. "An electrical fire? Did my kiln do this?"

He shrugs. "We need to investigate."

"You're hedging. You do think my kiln is to blame."

"We need to investigate," he repeats.

I fist my hands on my hips. "River Atlas Alston, I remember when you thought throwing your dirty diaper at a girl at the playground was the funniest joke you ever heard of. You better tell me the truth right this minute or I'm phoning your mom."

He grins. "Mom's been drinking champagne at the wedding reception all night."

He thinks he can outdo me? He has another thing coming.

"I guess I'll ring Sage and tell her about you and your wife's little secret."

His head rears back. "How do you know? We just found out."

"River. River. River. Never buy a pregnancy test within a thirty-mile radius of Winter Falls."

"Crap. Bessie will kill me if the gossip gals find out before she tells her family."

"All you have to do is tell me the truth and I'll forget all about your secret."

He frowns. "We don't have all the facts yet."

"Stop repeating yourself. I want to hear what *you* think happened."

He blows out a breath. "I think the kiln had a faulty wire and started the fire."

I stumble backwards and Brody catches me. "Easy, Soleil."

"Easy? How can I be easy?" I wail. "This is all my fault! I should have replaced the kiln."

Brody bends over until his face is mere inches from mine. "Did you know the kiln had a faulty wire?"

"No."

"How would you know to replace it if you didn't know about the faulty wire?"

I chew on my bottom lip instead of answering.

"You wouldn't, would you?"

I try River's line. "I need to investigate."

"Nope." Brody shakes his head. "I'm not allowing you to accept responsibility for a fire you didn't cause."

"You're not allowing me?" I hiss at him. "You don't own me, Brody Bragg."

"Pixie, I don't want to own you, but I do want you to let me in."

River clears his throat and I glance over at him. "We'll gather up our equipment and gear and be out of here within the next five to ten minutes."

"Thanks, River." I fling myself at him. "Thanks for saving my house."

He pats my back. "You're welcome."

I release him. "And I promise not to tell anyone about you-know-what. I would never reveal someone's secret."

"I expect you to babysit."

I ignore the burn in my stomach – *I'm not jealous of my friends. I'm not jealous of my friends* – and force a smile on my face. "Of course. Whenever you need me, I'll be there."

"You'll need to stay away from the shed until we finish our investigation."

I scowl. "Stay away from the shed? What about my pottery?"

"I hate to say this but there's nothing left."

"Not one single piece?"

"Sorry." He pats my shoulder before strolling off to where the rest of the firefighters are rolling up hoses and picking up gear.

"What am I going to do? I have orders to fill. I can't survive off the earnings of my knitted vibrator covers and honey products."

Brody wraps an arm around my shoulders and draws me near. "I got you. I can cover the expenses for a few months while you rebuild."

"I don't want you to spend all your savings on me."

"I've got the money. Don't worry."

I twist my neck to look up at him. "You do? Since when." But then I remember. "Oh, right. You have a trust fund from when your dad passed away."

"Yeah. Sure. The trust fund." He glances away as if he's lying.
"You need your sleep. You have a lot to deal with."

"I need to phone the insurance company, I need to purchase a new kiln, I need to contact all my customers who—"

He places a finger over my lips. "Tomorrow. Rest first."

"But—"

"It's after midnight. You can't call anyone now anyway."

Damn. He's right. "Fine. Bed it is."

Chapter 17

When did Soleil install curtains in her bedroom? ~ Message from Sage on the Winter Falls Facebook page

BRODY

I usher Soleil into the house.

"Go on," I say as I nudge her toward the bedroom. "Get ready for bed. I'll check the house is locked up."

"Thanks," she mutters as she trudges down the hallway.

Fuck. I run a hand down my face. I can't believe her pottery shed burned down. I wish I could erase all of the pain she's suffering now, but I can't. The best I can do is be there for her. Catch her when she stumbles and support her until she's back on her feet.

I walk around the house checking the doors and windows are locked. I'm not in a hurry as I want to give Soleil the chance to get into bed. I know I should sleep in my pillow fort in the spare bedroom, but I'm not letting her be alone. Not tonight.

When I finally enter Soleil's room, I nearly swallow my tongue at what I see. Soleil is standing in the middle of the room wearing nothing but her bra and panties.

"What-what." I clear my throat and try again. "What are you doing?"

"I need you, Brody."

"Whatever you need, I'm here, pixie."

She bites her lip. "I need you to make me forget."

Is she saying what I think she's saying?

"Make me forget, Brody."

I hesitate.

"Make love to me."

My cock nearly jumps out of my pants. He's ready and has no reservations.

"You've had a shit night. I don't want you to regret being with me."

"I promise not to regret it."

Easier said than done in my experience.

"Please. Don't make me beg."

If we're doing this, she's going to beg. She doesn't know it yet, but she'll find out soon enough.

"Just for tonight."

I want more than one night, but I'm helpless to deny her anything. She holds all the power.

"If we do this." She smiles. "I said if." She coughs to cover up her smile. "Then, you will listen to me and follow my directions."

Heat flares in her eyes and she shivers. "Okay," she breathes out.

Fucking hell. She's perfect. Perfect for me in every sense of the word. My cock agrees judging by how he presses against my zipper. Her gaze drops to my crotch and she licks her lips. I want those lips on me but not tonight. I'll wait until she realizes who she is to me before we go there.

I cross to her and palm her neck to bring her near before smashing my lips to hers. I drink her in. She tastes of the champagne she was drinking tonight. I don't need champagne. I could get drunk on her taste alone. I don't take my fill – I will never have my fill – but I do slow the kiss until I can step away from her.

She resembles a goddess standing there with her lips swollen and her eyes full of passion. My goddess.

"Clothes off. On the bed. On your knees."

She hesitates.

"If we're doing this, we're doing it my way." I drag a finger down her face. "Do you want to do this?"

She nods.

"Clothes off. On the bed."

She holds my gaze as she reaches around and unsnaps her bra. It falls to the floor and I clench my jaw to stop myself from moaning. I can't wait to get my hands and mouth on those rosy nipples. Soon. I promise myself.

She shimmies out of her underwear. I'm happy to note she's not cleanshaven. I prefer a woman who's natural. Who's all woman.

The sight causes my cock to twitch. I reach down and squeeze the base as hard as I can. Soleil's breath hitches in response.

"On the bed," I growl. "On your knees."

This time she doesn't hesitate to follow my orders. She climbs onto the bed and gets on her hands and knees in the middle. I undress before laying on my back under her.

"Widen your legs."

My cock jumps when she once again follows my orders without question. I said it once, but I'll say it again – fucking perfect for me. I scoot up the bed until I'm right where I want to be.

"I'm going to eat your pussy until you scream my name. Then, I'm going to fuck you until you forget your name."

Her entire body shivers. "Yes, please."

I dig my fingers into her ass cheeks and bring her pussy to my mouth. She goes to her elbows and I smack her ass.

"Did I say you can go to your elbows?"

"No."

"Do as I say or I'm going to stop."

"O-o-okay." Her voice trembles but I notice excitement leak from her core. She's into everything we're doing. I bet I can make her come at record speed. Time to find out.

My hands mold and squeeze her ass while I place kisses along her inner thighs until I'm nearly at her core. Then, I retreat and nibble along the skin of her thigh again until she's squirming underneath of me.

"Don't move," I growl.

I gently lick around her outer lips as I work my way toward her clit. Her thighs tremble and I know she's doing her best not to squirm for me.

"Good girl," I mutter against her skin.

I circle her clit with my tongue as a reward and she groans. Good response but I want her screaming my name. I circle her clit again. This time she grunts with frustration.

"You taste fantastic, pixie girl. I could lick your pussy all day long."

"But you're not licking it," she growls.

This time I slap her ass twice in quick succession.

"Who's in charge here?"

"You are."

"Who controls when you come?"

"You do."

"Someone's a quick learner," I mumble before latching onto her clit and sucking it hard. This time her moan is long and loud. That's more like it.

I slide my hands up her torso until I reach her breasts. I knead the plump beauties while I alternate nibbling on her outer lips with sucking on her clit and circling it with my tongue.

Her legs quiver and I know she's getting close. I move away from her clit and spear her core with my tongue.

"Brody," she moans.

I pluck at her nipples. "Scream my name when you come, pixie girl."

I thrust in and out of her core with my tongue. I wasn't lying. She tastes fantastic. I could do this all day long. My cock straining to reach the promised land calls me a liar but I ignore him. It's not his turn yet.

Soleil's thighs freeze and she shouts, "Yes," as she comes all over my tongue.

I don't wait for her climax to finish before pulling away from her and getting to my knees behind her.

I plunge into her and her walls clamp down on me. Fuck. She feels fantastic. I have to grit my teeth before I come. I am not some damn untried teenager. I will show Soleil I'm a man by making her climax again.

I press my hand on her shoulders. "Turn to the side. Cheek on the bed."

Her arms give out and she falls face first onto the bed. "Holy crap."

"I believe you mean holy Brody," I say as I slowly withdraw.

Once only the tip remains inside her, I pause.

"Please."

Exactly what I was waiting for. I reward her by plunging into her.

"Yes," she moans.

"Brody," I correct as I retreat.

I try to maintain my calm but I'm buried deep in Soleil. The place I've wanted to be for months. The place I've dreamed about, whacked off to, worried I'd never be.

Soon enough I'm pumping in and out of her like a man possessed. I fist her hair in my hand and lean my body over hers.

"You going to come again for me, pixie girl?"

"Y-y-yes?"

"Are you asking me? I ask the questions here. Are. You. Going. To. Come. Again?"

"Yes!" she snarls.

I bite her earlobe and her back arches in response. "Then, fucking come."

Her walls immediately clamp down on me as she climaxes. "Brody!"

Finally. There's the shout I was waiting for. I thrust in and out of her as she rides her orgasm. As soon as it wanes, I take what I want. I pound into her until I can hold back no longer.

My balls tingle and I let go. "Soleil," I moan as I finish.

I collapse on top of her but quickly roll off before I squash my little pixie.

"I wasn't too rough with you, was I?" I ask once my breathing slows down enough for me to talk.

"Nope. Just perfect."

My heart warms. *Perfect.* I want to be perfect for her. I open my mouth to tease her but she lets out a snore. I guess I fucked her to sleep. Good. She needs her sleep.

I force myself to stand and walk to the bathroom where I grab a washcloth and warm it before returning to the bed. As I'm cleaning her up, I jolt with realization.

Shit. We didn't use a condom. A condom never even occurred to me. I don't forget to wrap up. Ever. Soleil is going to be pissed.

I throw the washcloth on the floor and climb into bed before wrapping my arms around her. She probably won't let me hold her again after my screw up. And I wouldn't blame her. I need to treat her like the princess she is. Not be careless with her safety.

Chapter 18

I SNUGGLE INTO MY pillow. No, not my pillow. Brody. The man who showed me how good sex can be last night. Talk about a dark horse.

Holy multiple orgasms! I wouldn't mind hopping on this particular dark horse for another ride. But I can't. Brody isn't for me. He needs someone to mother him and I don't have the bandwidth to add a partner to the list of people I take care of.

Brody squeezes my hip. "What are you thinking about so hard this early in the morning?"

"My pottery shed, insurance, clients. My whole life falling apart."

I actually wasn't thinking of any of those things. I sure the hell am now, though. Holy crap. What am I going to do?

He rolls on top of me. "Don't worry, Soleil. We'll figure it out."

"We? There is no we."

I shove at him. He scowls but rolls off of me.

"I thought our status changed after last night."

I glare at him. "I told you it was just for last night."

"Our chemistry is off the charts. I vote we explore where this goes."

I can't deny the chemistry comment, because he's right. The two of us in bed together was explosive. But it can never be more.

"Good thing I have veto power because we are not exploring anything."

"Why am I not surprised?"

"Maybe because I've been telling you from day one, I don't want you."

He snorts. "You want me. But you don't want to want me."

"Whatever," I mumble as I climb out of bed.

I feel vulnerable being nude in front of him after telling him I don't want more from him, but I refuse to let it bother me. I grab a t-shirt from the drawer and put it on.

"There's something you should know."

I pause at the entrance to the bathroom. "What?"

"I didn't use a condom last night."

I whirl around to face him. "What?"

"I didn't use a condom last night," he repeats.

"What the hell, Brody? This is why we can never have a relationship. You're immature and selfish."

He springs out of bed and stalks toward me. "I think I proved I'm not immature or selfish last night."

I keep my gaze firmly planted on his face. I will not look down. I will not look down. "Except you didn't use a condom."

"I could have lied. I could have kept it to myself and never told you. But I didn't."

He has a point, but I'm not done being angry. "You never asked me if you could enter me bare."

"As I recall, you were begging for my cock."

I narrow my eyes on him. "I do not beg."

He tucks a strand of hair behind my ear. "Pixie, you do, too."

I bat his hand away. "I refuse to discuss this."

"I apologize for not using a condom. I promise I'm clean. I haven't been with anyone since I moved to Winter Falls a few months ago. But if you want me to, I'll get tested. Scratch that. I'll get tested anyway."

Damn it. There he goes again. Poking holes in my 'you're an immature man-child' argument.

"I'm clean, too," I say. "And I'm on the pill."

"Now we've cleared that up. Let's return to the discussion of us."

"Do you have short-term memory problems? I told you. There is no us. There will never be an us."

He steps closer until his heat surrounds me. "Why not?"

"I don't have time for this. I have a ton of shit to deal with today. You're not on my to-do list."

He smirks. "Oh, pixie, you're always on my to-do list."

I shove him away. "I'm serious, Brody. My life is crumbling. And there's no one here to pick up the pieces. It's always me picking up everyone else's pieces."

"Whoa. Hold on. I'm here. I'm willing to help out however you need me to."

"You!" I shriek. "The same person who can't clean up his mess on the dining room table? The same person who thinks it's funny to dress a goat up as a princess? The same person who set his bed on fire practicing for some prank?"

"One, the mess is my work. Two, the princess goat was freaking hilarious. And, three, I've apologized about the bed and ordered you a new one."

"You don't get it, do you? I take care of everyone. I don't have the time or energy to take care of you, too."

"I'm not asking you to. I can take care of myself."

I snort. "Which is why you've found somewhere else to live."

"You want me to leave, I'm gone."

"You're missing the point."

"What is the point?"

"I want someone to take care of me," I shout. "I want someone who thinks of me first. Not someone who expects me to drop out of college to care for them."

Brody grasps my hand and leads me back to bed. He picks me up and sets me in the bed before crawling in beside me. "I think you need to explain yourself."

"I need to phone the insurance company," I argue but even I can admit my argument sounds pretty lame.

"They don't open until eight and it's not yet seven. You have time."

I grunt because he's right, but I'll be damned if I admit it out loud.

He squeezes my hand. "I think I deserve an explanation."

"An explanation about what?" I ask despite knowing exactly what he means. Crap. I'm the one acting childish now.

He ignores my snippiness. "Who made you drop out of college? Who made you feel as if you have to take care of everyone?"

I fiddle with the comforter. "My mom."

He sucks in a breath. "Your mom didn't look after you?"

"She did. Or, at least, she tried. But she couldn't take care of me." I stop my explanation there. I don't want to continue.

"I have all day to sit here and pry answers out of you."

"I don't."

"Then, get to talking."

"Fine." I cross my arms over my chest and stare at the wall as I explain. "My mom got cancer when I was twelve. My dad was useless. Probably because he was younger than her and she had always taken care of his every need up until then. Anyway, I had to step up and handle the house and care for Mom. While he was off working and avoiding the situation, I was here cleaning up her puke, feeding her crackers, taking care of the house, and making dinner."

"You were twelve," he grumbles. I know exactly how old I was.

"It was all worth it because she beat the cancer. That's what we thought at least. I went off to art school in Denver thinking everything was fine. It wasn't. The cancer came back. Dad visited me at my apartment in Denver and begged me to come home. He said Mom needed me. What he meant was he needed someone to come home and take care of everything because he wouldn't."

"I quit school, packed up all my belongings, and came home. This round of cancer was way worse. Or maybe I was older and could understand it better. I don't know. What I do know is by the time Mom was better, my year deferment from college had passed."

"You didn't go back?"

"I tried. But my heart wasn't in it. I couldn't bear to be away from my mom. She lived for two more years before the cancer came back. She wasn't interested in fighting it this time."

He wipes a tear from my face. "I'm sorry, pixie. I didn't know your mom had passed."

"I should be over it by now," I say as tears stream down my face.

He scowls. "Who says?"

"It's been more than a decade."

He palms my neck and forces me to face him. "There is no time limit on grief. Your feelings are your feelings. No one can tell you what to feel."

I swipe at the moisture on my face. "When did you get to be this smart?"

He puffs out his chest. "I've always been this smart."

"Dork," I say but there's no snark in my voice.

"Where's your dad now?"

I scowl. "He left. He wasn't a native of Winter Falls the way Mom was. He didn't ever feel as if he fit in here."

"Do you have any contact with him?"

"Not really. He has a new life with a new wife. Another woman who's older than him and babies him."

"I'm sorry, pixie."

I blow out a breath. "And now you understand why we can't be a couple."

His brow wrinkles. "I do?"

I roll my eyes. "Duh. I'm done taking care of people who can't care for themselves."

"I can take care of myself."

"Sure, you can."

"And I'm pretty sure I took care of you last night, too."

My body heats as memories of last night flash into my mind. Him going all alpha and ordering me around. I got off on it. Big time.

"Sex is sex. I need a man who can take care of me all the time," I say as I climb out of the bed. "You're too young."

"If you give me the chance, I'll not only take care of you but I'll treat you like a princess," he claims. When I don't answer, he sighs. "Please think about it."

I wish I could believe him. I wish he could be the man for me. The man I want. The one to take care of me.

But, no, he's Brody, the prankster.

I'm afraid he's just like my dad. Going after an older woman to take care of him so he can do whatever he wants without any responsibilities.

I can't chance it.

Chapter 19

BRODY

Riley glances up from his workbench where he's staining a piece of wood when I walk into his garage. "No."

My twin is a handyman slash woodworker. The pieces he makes are pretty awesome. When he sets up a booth at a Winter Falls' festival, he always sells out the first morning.

Unfortunately, I don't have any of his talent with tools. Give me a keyboard and I can run circles around him. But tools? I didn't know the difference between a shovel and a trowel until recently.

"You don't even know what I'm going to ask."

"The last time you asked for a favor you spilled an entire can of stain. No."

"It was an accident."

"What about the time you thought it'd be funny to rearrange my tools? It took me a week to put things back in place."

"You shouldn't have told Mr. Barker who stole his boxers."

"You didn't need his boxers."

"How else was I going to dress the scarecrow?"

He rolls his eyes. "You could have used your own boxers."

"But we set the scarecrow on fire." It was seriously awesome.

"You could have sweet talked Mom into buying you a new pair of boxers."

"You're the sweet talker. Not me."

It's true. My brother can charm the pants off anyone. Although, nowadays the only woman he's charming is Moon.

He smirks. "It's true. I am the charming twin."

"Will the charming twin please lend me some tools?"

"Tools? Do you know what tools are?"

I motion to the wall behind him. "A tool is a device or implement, especially one held in the hand, used to carry out a particular function."

"Being able to quote a definition from the dictionary doesn't mean you have the first clue on how to use a tool."

"I didn't say otherwise."

"What do you need tools for anyway?"

"I'm going to build a shed."

After Soleil told me she needed a man to take care of her, I sat down and thought about how I could go about taking care of her. Because I am not losing her. The sex last night merely served to confirm what I thought before – we're perfect together.

Which is why I came up with a plan to rebuild her shed. I could just buy her a shed or hire someone to build one, but I need to show her I'm the one taking care of her personally with my own hands. And I don't want her to have to wait for the insurance payout to build. Who knows when that will happen?

Riley feigns cleaning his ear. "I think I misheard you. Because you couldn't possibly have said you're going to build a shed. Not my brother who thinks playing a videogame is work."

I shove aside the hurt his comment about video games causes to explain, "I'm rebuilding Soleil's pottery shed."

He bursts out laughing. "You. I can't." He struggles for breath as he continues to laugh.

I cross my arms over my chest and wait him out. I knew his response wouldn't be favorable. But I came here today prepared to beg for help. I'll do anything for Soleil including spending the rest of my days being made fun of by my brothers. My brothers would make fun of me no matter what anyway.

He grabs his phone. "What are you doing?" I ask.

"Messaging everyone."

I scowl. "What about twin powers? And helping a twin out?"

"This is too good not to share."

"What's too good not to share?" Elder asks as he strolls into the garage.

I spin around to confront him and notice he's not alone. His twin Miller is with him. "What are you doing here?"

"We came to check up on you."

I roll my eyes. "Seriously. What are you doing here?" I address Miller since he can't lie for shit.

When he grunts in response, I exit the garage and survey the area. I bet those gossip gals are behind this. I don't know how they do it, but they seem to know everything happening in town. Sometimes before it happens.

"I came as fast as I could," Peace says as he hurries toward the garage. Great. The Bragg bunch is complete. "What's the emergency?"

"Emergency?" I ask.

"Riley sent a 9-1-1 family meeting text."

I rub a hand down my face. Having five brothers is a pain in my ass.

"Brody thinks he's going to build a shed," Riley says.

I scowl at him. "I don't think I'm going to build a shed. I *am* going to build a shed."

"The last time you helped out at Moon's diner you asked me what a Philip's screwdriver is."

"I'm willing to learn."

Riley props his hands on his hips. "I blame those DIY television programs. All those people buying houses and renovating them despite not having a clue what they're doing. They make it seem as if anyone can renovate a house."

"If you watched until the end, you'd know they do manage to renovate the house," I point out.

"Why do you want to build a shed?" Elder asks.

"I bet it's to replace Soleil's pottery shed since it burned down last night," Peace says.

"Fuck," Miller grumbles. "Her shed burned down?"

"Yeah. With all of her pottery in it."

Which is why she needs a new shed pronto. She has a ton of pottery to re-make since all the pottery stored in her shed was already bought by customers and waiting to be shipped out.

Luckily, she can work at the community center in the meantime but apparently the kiln there is much smaller.

"How about this? We'll all help," Riley suggests.

I wish I could accept their help. With the five of us working on the shed, we'd be done in no time. But I can't accept their help. I have to do this on my own. I have to show Soleil *I* can take care of her. Not my brothers and me. Me.

"I have to do this on my own," I say.

"Why?"

"It's for Soleil."

I'm not explaining how I need to care for Soleil on my own. I'm not telling them about her background. It's private. I'm honored and privileged that she told me her secrets.

"This is going to be fun." Elder rubs his hands together. "I need to contact Sage and place my bet. I'm winning Project Cub."

"You haven't placed your bet yet?" Riley asks.

Peace raises his hand. "I did."

Miller grunts in agreement.

If they think they can rile me up by talking smack about placing bets about when Soleil and I finally get together, they can think again. I don't give a shit what anyone else thinks about the two of us and our relationship. The only person I care about is Soleil.

Elder grins. "Why did the builder shy away from making construction jokes?" No one guesses. We never do. "Because the joke still needed some work."

Elder's the jokester amongst the brothers. Unfortunately, his jokes are usually the equivalent of dad jokes. Everyone ignores him since we're used to him.

"We're not going to seriously let Brody do this on his own?" Riley asks. "Winter Falls doesn't have an emergency room."

"I don't need an emergency room. I need to borrow your tools."

"You don't have the first clue how to build a shed."

"I downloaded a plan."

He chuckles. "Of course, you did. All questions can be answered by the internet."

I ignore his dig on my obsession with computers and the internet. "I have a list of tools I need. I can buy them but I thought it would be a waste to purchase them since I probably won't use them again once the shed is built."

"Buy them?" He cocks a brow. "Do you realize how much tools cost? They're not cheap."

"I can lend you some money," Elder offers, and Miller grunts in agreement.

"I don't need anyone's money. I need to borrow some tools. Nothing more. Nothing less."

"What about the other supplies – lumber, shingles, windows, a door? The list goes on and on. Building a shed is not a cheap endeavor," Riley says.

"Especially if you want to insulate it so Soleil can work on her pottery in the winter," Peace adds.

I open my mouth to tell them I've got plenty of money but snap it shut again when I remember it's not time. Not yet. I'll tell them about my business and the money I've earned as soon as it's a success.

"I made a budget," I say instead of showing them the balance in my bank account.

"You certain you can afford to do this on your own?" Riley asks.

I grit my teeth. I hate how my brothers treat me like a baby. Even Riley who's barely two minutes older than me.

"I'm certain."

Elder grins. "Please say we can at least watch."

"I don't care what you do as long as you don't tell Soleil about the shed."

"How are you going to keep it a secret?" Miller asks.

"I'm going to tell her there's an ongoing arson investigation and she isn't allowed near the site."

Peace nods. "Good idea. I'll spread the word around town."

"Thanks, half-Bragg. You're not half bad."

"Don't make me change my mind."

I bat my eyelashes. "I wouldn't dare."

"Where's your list of tools?" Riley asks.

I smile as I hand it to him.

"You need to promise you'll let me know if you get in over your head."

I don't hesitate. "I promise."

I'm not an idiot. I may want to build this shed on my own, but I also want Soleil to have a shed she can use. If I need my brothers, I know they'll be there. They'll razz me the whole time, but they'll be there.

Chapter 20

THUMP!

My eyes fly open at the sound of a thud. Is someone in the house? Do I have a burglar? I reach across the bed to nudge Brody awake but he's not there. He hasn't been there since the morning after we had sex.

It's as it should be. Brody sleeping in the same bed as me will lead to us doing other things – sexy, sweaty things – in this bed. Which is wrong. I would be using him since I have no plans to be in a relationship with him.

Someone groans. Oh no. Is Brody hurt? Has he been attacked?

I jump out of bed and rush to the door. *Hold on, Soleil.* Grab a weapon first. I reach for my baseball bat but it's not there. Shit. What else can I use as a weapon? I scan the room but there's nothing here. I can hardly defend myself from an attacker with a pillow.

I pick up the one thing that could possibly help. A lamp. I yank on the cord until the plug comes out of the wall. *Okay, Soleil.* Here we go.

I open the door and sneak out of my room with the lamp raised. I creep down the hallway while listening for an intruder but I don't hear anything other than Brody's light moan.

I reach the living room and scan the area. A light flips on and I scream.

"I've got a weapon and I know how to use it!"

Brody raises his hands in surrender. "I'm unarmed."

"Where's the intruder?"

"What intruder?"

"The one who hit you."

"An intruder hit me?"

"There was a thud and then you moaned."

"Because I fell off the sofa."

I set my weapon on the dining room table. "Are you okay? Did you hurt yourself?"

He chuckles. "Does hurting my pride count?"

I snatch two glasses from the cupboard and pour water into them before handing one to Brody. "You're certain you didn't hurt yourself? You were moaning awful loud."

"I hit my head on the coffee table when I fell."

I set my water down before grasping his head to check it. I notice a trickle of blood on his temple. "You're bleeding."

"It's no—"

I don't let him finish. I capture his hand and drag him down the hallway, through my bedroom to my bathroom. I indicate the toilet. "Sit."

"But I don't need to go potty."

I growl at him. "You're bleeding. This is no joking matter."

He sobers. "Sorry. No more jokes."

I find a washcloth and wet it before kneeling in front of him to clean the blood. His eyes sparkle and I wag my finger at him.

"We agreed no jokes."

"What about sexual innuendos? Do they count as jokes?"

"You can't help yourself, can you?"

I press the cloth against his wound and he jerks back. "So much for not being hurt."

"It's barely a scratch. I don't want you taking care of me."

A fist wraps around my heart and squeezes. He doesn't want me to take care of him? I can't deny how much those words hurt. This is what I do. I take care of the people I care for. Does he not want to be a person I care for? I thought—

"Whatever you're thinking – stop."

I scowl at him. "You don't know what I'm thinking."

"I didn't say I did. But I do know whatever you're thinking is wrong."

"How do you know what I'm thinking is wrong if you don't know what I'm thinking?"

He cups my chin. "Because hurt flashed in your eyes at my words. I didn't mean to hurt you."

"You didn't hurt me."

"Pixie, don't lie to me."

His blue eyes staring into mine are full of honesty and warmth and – damn it – I can't lie to him.

"I want you to care for me but I don't want you to take care of me," he says.

I narrow my eyes at him. How does he know what I was thinking?

He brushes my hair from my forehead. "I know you, Soleil. You can deny it all you want, but I do."

Denying him is exactly what I want to do, but I can't since he called me on it. I do the next best thing. I lean back, forcing him to drop his hand.

"Maybe we should concentrate on getting your wound clean. A head wound is no joke," I say as I resume cleaning the blood from his temple.

"This isn't a head wound. A head wound is when you end up dizzy and puking your guts out."

"Are you speaking from experience?"

"Never challenge Riley to a diving competition."

"Why not?"

"He's a big fat cheater who'll push you off the diving board to win."

"And you hit your head?"

"Nothing clears out the municipal pool faster than a kid throwing up in it."

"Thanks for the visual."

He grins. "You're welcome."

"You're such a dork."

"A charming dork."

I snort. "Charming?"

"Okay. Fine. Sexy dork. I didn't want to say it and make you feel uncomfortable, but there you have it."

"You have no filter."

"Why would I have a filter? I'm not a swimming pool."

"A brain to mouth filter to prevent every single idea you have from popping out of your mouth," I clarify.

"Sounds boring."

There's no reasoning with Brody. I concentrate on cleaning the blood from his face. "I think it stopped bleeding."

"Thanks for being such a wonderful nurse. Too bad you didn't wear your naughty nurse uniform."

"How do you know about my naughty nurse uniform?"

He swallows. "You have a naughty nurse uniform?"

I giggle. "Got you."

"You're beautiful when you laugh."

Butterflies long dormant in my stomach threaten to awaken at his words. Not happening. Brody is too young for me. Just like my dad was way too young for my mom.

I turn away from him and the warmth in those baby blue eyes. There's a limit to how much temptation a woman can handle before she breaks. Especially since I know how good he kisses. How skilled he is at giving me orgasms.

I dig the first aid kit out from underneath the sink and set it on the vanity. I remove some antiseptic wipes and a bandage before kneeling in front of him again.

I pause with my hand poised above his wound with an antiseptic wipe. "This may sting a bit."

"As long as you kiss it to make it feel better."

"You're incorrigible."

"What a weird way to say I'm sexy."

I clean the wound and place the bandage over it. "There. All done."

He pats his lips. "Except for a kiss."

I roll my eyes and stand. "You don't have to sleep on the sofa."

"The sofa's fine."

"Which is why you fell off and hurt yourself."

"We're telling everyone I got this cut while I was saving you from a ghost."

I groan. "Please don't dress up as a ghost again."

He grins. "But how else can I save you?"

I slap his chest and he captures my hand. "I don't need saving."

He rubs his thumb along the pulse point of my inner wrist and I inhale a deep breath before I melt into a pool of hormones at his feet. Maybe I do need saving after all.

"And I can sleep on the sofa."

"I feel bad. You're too tall for my sofa. Just sleep in the bed."

"I can't sleep in the bed with you."

I jerk my hand away from him. "Why not? Do I have cooties now?"

"You definitely don't have cooties unless cooties mean you're super sexy and difficult to resist."

"We'll build another wall between us."

"No need, pixie. I'm sleeping on the sofa."

"But—"

He presses a finger against my lips to quiet me. "There's no way I can sleep in a bed with your sexy ass knowing how you taste and feel."

"A man should be able to control himself."

"I can control myself fine. But laying next to you smelling your honey scent and not being able to touch you is torture."

My mouth drops open. "Oh."

"Until you're ready to let me back in, I'll be on the sofa."

Ready to let him back in? Not happening.

"What if I'm never ready?"

"Then, I'll sleep on your sofa forever." He tucks a stray hair behind my ear before kissing my forehead. "Sleep well, pixie girl."

He saunters away without another word. When he's gone, I can finally breathe again. Phew. I was sorely tempted to invite him back into my bed for more than sleeping. But I can't. He's not the man for me. He's too immature.

Except he wasn't acting very immature tonight. He must have known all he had to do was push a tiny bit and I would have given in and had sex with him. But he didn't push. He walked away. Maybe Brody is more mature than I give him credit for.

Chapter 21

BRODY

I spread the plans for the shed out on the picnic table in Soleil's backyard. I've spent the past week cleaning up the space and removing the debris. It's finally time to start building.

The first thing I need to do is assemble a floor frame and then add the floor sheeting. I study the plans for a few minutes until I have the instructions memorized. And then I begin.

It's not long before I'm sweating my ass off. I pull off my t-shirt and throw it on the table.

"Sexy thing!"

I whirl around to yell at my twin and notice he's not alone. The entire Bragg bunch is setting up lawn chairs in Soleil's backyard.

"What are you doing here?"

"Isn't it obvious?" Riley asks as he sits in his chair.

"I think it's obvious." Elder pops open a beer.

"Completely obvious." Peace sips on his beer.

Miller grunts in agreement.

I join them and reach into the cooler. I could use a beer, too. It's been a long day. I woke up early to finish coding my new game before coming out back to spend the afternoon building the shed.

Riley slaps my hand. "No beer if you're using power tools."

Peace groans. "Can you imagine Brody drinking tequila and using power tools?"

I scowl. "I would never drink tequila and use power tools."

What do they think of me? I'm not a child. I understand safety protocols.

Elder snorts. "The same way you would never drink tequila and break into someone's house again."

Riley shivers. "Thanks for the visual. As if I need a reminder of someone's balls in my face."

I ignore my twin. "First of all, I didn't break into anyone's house. It was a library."

Elder rolls his eyes. "This time."

"Second, I never promised not to break into houses again."

"I don't understand what Cassandra was thinking allowing you to drink tequila," Peace grumbles.

"Cassandra owns the only bar in town. Of course, she served me tequila. It's her livelihood. Besides, it's not illegal for me to drink tequila."

Peace frowns. "Obviously, an oversight on my part. I'll bring it up at the next city council meeting."

I glare at him. "There is no city council."

He grins. "I can ask the chief of police to make a town ordinance."

"And I can ring your wife and let her know you're trying to make it illegal for someone in town to drink."

He scowls. "Olivia would jump on the bandwagon and before we knew what was happening all kinds of drugs would be legal in town."

I grin. "I know."

His wife is a troublemaker. They're hilarious together. He's all 'the law is the law' and she's all 'the law is open to interpretation'. Freaking hilarious.

Peace throws his arms in the air. "Fine. You win. Drink tequila whenever you want."

"Whoa! Whenever he wants?" Riley asks. "Are you bored at your job? Because you're asking for trouble."

"I'm not going to drink tequila whenever I want."

Do I go a little crazy when I drink tequila? Yes, I admit I do. But it's not as if I'm doing shots at lunchtime every day. I can control myself.

Observe how I've kept my hands and mouth off of Soleil since the night I fell off of the sofa. And I know a little nudge from me was all I needed to get her to agree to have sex with me.

But did I nudge? No, I did not. I let her nurse me and then I went back to the sofa where I programmed software in my mind until my dick went soft.

"Does Brody have a boo-boo?" Riley asks and I realize I'm rubbing my hand over the bandage. I drop my hand but the damage is already done.

My brothers stand as a group and approach. I retreat but they circle me. Damn. I'm surrounded.

"What happened?" Riley glares at me. "You didn't break one of my tools, did you?"

Of course, he's worried about his precious tools. Who cares about the well-being of his twin?

"I didn't break a tool."

"If you didn't break a tool, what did you do?" Elder asks. "Walk into a wall?"

"I have never walked into a wall," I huff.

He cocks an eyebrow.

"You shoved me into the wall. It's not the same thing."

He shrugs. "Pretty sure you tripped."

"On what? Your foot when you stuck it out before pushing me?"

He smiles. "You still tripped."

"I am not looking forward to having sons. Give me a daughter any day," Peace says, and everyone's attention switches to him.

"Are you and Olivia trying?" I ask.

"Not officially but I caught Olivia throwing away her birth control pills the other day."

I chuckle. "I guess you're trying."

He crosses his arms over his chest. "I think she wants to get pregnant before we're married, the little troublemaker."

"Are you going to knock her up?"

He smirks. "I'm trying my best."

"Me too," Miller grumbles.

Elder rubs his hands together. "We should bet on who gets pregnant first."

Miller sizes Peace up. "I got this."

"Because you can control whether your sperm fertilizes one of Eden's eggs?" Peace asks.

"Yep."

"Did you skip sex education in school? We have excellent sex education in Winter Falls."

Miller crosses his arms over his chest. "I think I have it figured out."

"If you two are done talking about having babies, can we get back to how Brody got his boo-boo?" Riley asks.

I go on the attack. My brothers will bust a gut if they find out I fell off the couch. "Boo-boo? How old are you?"

Riley rocks back on his heels. "Older than you."

"By two minutes," I remind him.

Elder rubs his knuckles over my head. "You'll always be the baby to us."

I bat his hands away. "Screw you."

"Such nasty language for a baby."

"I'm not a fucking baby," I growl.

Peace taps the bandage on my temple. "And yet you have a boo-boo on your head."

"Anyone can get a head injury."

"Head injury?" Miller asks.

I'm done discussing this. I need to get back to work. This shed is not going to build itself.

"I fell. There, are you happy now?"

I start to walk away but Miller blocks me. "How?"

I avoid the question. "Is no one in this family on my side?"

Riley chuckles. "You know the deal. When you're in the pre-mating phase, you're on your own."

"The pre-mating phase? Are you a sociologist now?"

"He's right," Elder says. "While you and Soleil are dancing around each other, you're equivalent to fresh meat at the market."

"I thought Harmony said you couldn't eat meat."

"Stop avoiding the question," Peace orders. "Tell us how you got hurt or I'll have a patrol car stop by Soleil's work and ask her."

"Soleil's not involved."

"I may be new to this whole brother thing, but I'm not an idiot. If she weren't involved, you would have told us already."

"She's not involved. Can we leave it now?"

Elder barks out a laugh. "If Soleil's not involved, he hurt himself doing something embarrassing. Let me guess. You fell in the bathtub while jerking off."

"What is your obsession with me and jerking off? No, I did not fall in the bathtub."

"Did you forget you had your headphones on when you walked away from your computer again?"

I sigh. "One time. I forgot my headphones one time." Probably because I've since bought wireless headphones.

Elder throws his hands in the air. "I give up. Tell us now."

Miller grunts in agreement.

I search for an escape, and Riley wags a finger at me. "Don't think you can run away. Your scrawny non-running ass wouldn't make it far."

"I am not scrawny." I refuse to be the runt of the Bragg litter. There's a reason I lift weights when I'm stuck on a coding problem.

"And Miller's biceps aren't the size of your waist either."

Miller flexes his biceps in case I get any ideas.

"Fine. I fell off the couch and hit my head on the coffee table. Are you happy now?"

Riley groans. "I'm not happy. I had you and Soleil getting together as a couple this week, which isn't going to happen if you're sleeping on the couch."

"Excellent. I'm winning this bet." Elder smiles. "What's the best way to lose some pounds? Have a gambling problem in the UK." He laughs at his own joke while everyone else groans.

"I swear his jokes are getting worse now he has a wife and daughter," I say.

"But I do have a wife and daughter while you're still working on your grand gesture." Elder motions toward the shed.

"I need to get back to it."

"This is disappointing," someone shouts. I groan when I notice who it is. The entire gossip gal crew has arrived.

"I thought they'd all be shirtless by now," Feather says.

"I told you we should wait until it warmed up," Cayenne says.

"Don't fight it. It only makes it worse," Peace whispers before strolling toward the group. "Ladies, how can I help you today?"

"By removing your shirt for starters," Clove demands.

"You're on your own." Elder strolls off and Miller follows him.

"Don't break any of my tools," Riley orders before leaving as well.

The gossip gals are now sitting in the chairs my brothers abandoned and Peace is nowhere to be seen.

"Don't mind us," Sage hollers. "We'll be as quiet as church mice."

I know a lost cause when I see it. I run a hand down my face before returning to my plans.

Chapter 22

MY BODY ACHES AS I walk home after yet another day of working at the community center. Don't get me wrong. I'm glad I have some equipment there so I can continue to work, but the kiln at the center is small. It's going to take me months to catch up with the outstanding orders I have. Orders I've already been paid for.

And there's no new money coming in until I catch up. Except for one buyer who is apparently willing to wait several months for her pottery. She's been buying a piece every single day since the fire. I've made a few of them but most of them are at the bottom of my very long to-do list.

I hear a buzz coming from inside my house as I climb the stairs. I groan. Great. Brody the prankster is up to no good. Again. So much for a relaxing evening with a glass of wine.

I stomp into my house, ready to lay into Brody, but freeze when it becomes clear what the noise is.

"What are you doing?"

Brody glances up from the vacuum cleaner and smiles at me. He speaks but I can't hear him over the vacuum.

"What?" I shout.

He switches off the vacuum. "Welcome home, Soleil."

"What did you break?"

His forehead wrinkles. "What did I break?"

"You must have broken something. Why else are you cleaning?"

"I'm cleaning because you don't have time to."

I narrow my eyes at him. "You didn't break anything?"

"Nope. Now, have you eaten?"

"Have I eaten? Did you seriously ask if I've eaten?"

He checks his watch. "It's after seven. Did you get something to eat with Moon at the diner before you came home?"

"Did I eat at the diner?"

"Let me put this away and then I'll heat up some food for you."

"Heat up some food for me?"

Why am I repeating everything he says? Probably because nothing he's saying makes sense. He's going to feed me?

"Don't look so surprised. Do you think the food fairies have been leaving you food in the refrigerator for the past week?"

I shrug. "I assumed you bought the food from the diner."

"Did you notice any take-out bags?"

I roll my eyes. "This is Winter Falls. There are no take-out bags. If you want to buy food to bring home, you need to bring your own dishes."

"I haven't been buying food from the diner. I've been cooking."

"You've been cooking?"

"Yes." He smiles. "And you've been eating the food I made. Unless you threw it away."

I wag my finger at him. "You don't throw food away in Winter Falls."

His nose scrunches. "I don't know. I threw away the first batch of chocolate chip cookies I made when they burnt to a crisp."

"They still should have gone on the compost pile."

He nods. "Lesson learned. No throwing food away. Even when you have to douse it with water to prevent a fire."

I groan. "I'm glad I wasn't here."

"I promise there wasn't a fire. And the next batch was way better. In fact," he scratches his chin, "I couldn't find the remaining cookies when I woke up the next morning."

I feel my cheeks warm. I inhaled those cookies after a long day at my kiln. "I plead the fifth."

"I'm glad you liked them. Hopefully, you'll enjoy my pasta bake casserole. I didn't have much time to cook today and all the recipe blogs recommended making casseroles when you're busy." He chatters on as he puts the vacuum cleaner away and strolls to the kitchen.

"It'll be fine," I say as I fall onto a bar stool. I'm certain whatever he cooked is edible. I'm just glad I don't have to cook. That someone cooked for me for a change.

"Fine?" he asks as he opens the oven and removes the pasta concoction.

The scent of melted cheese and marinara sauce hits me and my stomach rumbles.

He sets the dish on the counter in front of me. "I'm hoping for better than fine."

I inhale another whiff of cheese and pasta. Comfort food at its best. "Smells good."

He hands me a plate, silverware, and a napkin. "Do you want a glass of wine or water?" he asks as he opens the fridge.

"A glass of water."

He sets a glass of water on the counter before scooping a huge helping of pasta and cheese onto my plate.

"Do you expect me to eat all of this?"

He wiggles his eyebrows. "If you don't finish your dinner, there will be no dessert for you."

I bite my bottom lip. "What's for dessert?"

His eyes flare. "Whatever you want, pixie girl."

My body warms at the idea of having him for dessert. The last time we had sex – the one and only time we had sex – I didn't get a chance to taste him.

Brody taps my plate. "Eat first. You need to eat. I know you've been skipping lunch every day."

I narrow my eyes on him. "How do you know I've been skipping lunch? Are you spying on me?"

He chuckles. "I don't need to. I get a report from the gossip gals every day about your behavior."

I drop my fork and it clangs as it hits my plate. "You have got to be kidding me."

He shrugs. "Small town living."

"I don't get a report about what you're doing every day."

"Probably because I work all day at home alone."

I pick my fork back up and point it at him. "If all you do is work, then why are you fidgeting in your chair?"

He cocks an eyebrow. "Seriously? You practically undressed me with your eyes and you're wondering why I'm fidgeting?"

"I didn't undress you with my eyes."

"Sure, you didn't." He nudges my fork. "Eat."

"What are you? The food police?" I grumble before stuffing a mound of pasta into my mouth.

"I want to take care of you."

I nearly choke on my food. He wants to take care of me? I'm the one who takes care of everyone. Not the other way around.

He thrusts my glass of water into my hands. "Drink this."

The water soothes my throat and I manage to swallow my food. I eat a few bites as I decide what to say.

"Uh oh. Here it comes," Brody mutters.

"Comes what?"

"Whatever bullshit you're going to sprout."

I glare at him. "I do not sprout bullshit."

"Okay." He motions toward me. "Let's hear this non-bull-shit."

"I don't want you to take care of me."

"I beg to disagree. You said you want a man who takes care of you." He indicates the food on the table. "Thus, I'm taking care of you."

"No. You can't be sweet."

He grins. "I think I've proven I can be incredibly sweet."

"I can't resist you when you're being sweet."

"Then, stop resisting me."

"But you're too young for me."

He growls. "I am not a fucking child. I think I proved I'm a man to you already but I'm ready and able to prove it to you again."

Every nerve ending in my body lights up. Those dormant butterflies flap their wings in my stomach and warmth spreads through me. Stop it. This is Brody. The man who doesn't hesitate to dress an animal up as a princess as a prank.

"You're immature."

"Immature? Cooking and cleaning for you all week because you've been busy and stressed out about your pottery shed burning down is immature?"

"The pranks."

"There's nothing wrong with having a bit of fun in your life." He stands and rounds the counter until he's right in front of me. He tucks a strand of hair behind my ear. "You deserve to have some fun in your life."

"Your definition of fun and mine are completely different."

He smirks. "I know one way we enjoy fun together."

My panties dampen as images of the fun night we spent together flash into my mind.

"We can't."

"Why not? Give me one reason. One good reason."

"I'm too old for you."

He frowns. "I'm not your dad. I don't want you because you're older and will take care of me. I want you because you're Soleil. Besides." He smirks. "Does this feel as if I'm too young for you?"

He smashes his lips to mine and I gasp. He doesn't hesitate and shoves his tongue into my mouth. He smells of sandalwood and tastes of man and musk. I can't get enough. I grasp his shoulders and pull him near.

I give in. I'm done fighting him. This. Whatever it is.

Chapter 23

BRODY

Soleil's honey taste drives me wild. My brain is screaming at me to get her to bed as quickly as possible. I manage to stop myself before I fling her over my shoulder and carry her to the bedroom. This woman deserves more than a quick and dirty fuck. She deserves the world.

I pull away from her lips before planting kisses along her jaw until I reach her ear. "Do you want me, pixie girl?"

She moans in response. I bite her ear. "I need to hear the words."

"Yes," she sighs. "I want you."

I sink my teeth into her neck and she moans as her head falls back and she arches into me. There's my girl. I lick and suck at the area until she's writhing beneath me. My cock presses against my zipper eager to get to the promised land.

I wrap my arms around her waist and lift her from the stool. She winds her legs around my hips. She wiggles her core against my cock and I tap her ass.

"Be good, pixie, or I won't let you come for a very, very long time."

Her breath hitches. Hmmm. Maybe I should tease her for a long time anyway. Ideas of the ways I can bring Soleil to the brink only to slow down again whirl in my mind as I carry her to the bedroom.

I lay her on the bed and stand to admire her. Her face is flushed and her hair is fanned out around the pillow. She reminds me of a sweet and innocent fairy. A fairy I'm ready to dirty up until she's screaming my name.

She reaches for the hem of her t-shirt, but I stop her.

"It's my job to undress you."

Her hands flop to her sides. "Get to it."

"Who's in charge here?"

Her eyes narrow in challenge for a moment before she clears her throat. "You. You're in charge."

"Which is exactly how you enjoy it, isn't it?"

"If I admit I enjoy a man who's in charge in the bedroom, will you get to taking charge?"

I chuckle. "What do you think?" I cross my arms over my chest.

She inhales a deep breath and lets it go. "You're in charge in the bedroom."

"And?"

"And I like it."

"Good girl." I kneel on the bed and crawl toward her.

"Can I touch you this time?"

I freeze with my hands on the hem of her t-shirt. "You want to touch me?" She nods. "You want your mouth on me?" Her eyes flare.

My cock pulses against my zipper. He is down with this idea.

"New plan." I clasp Soleil's hand and help her off the bed. "Any chance you have handcuffs somewhere?"

Her eyes flare. "No."

I wink. "We'll make do."

I reach for the hem of her t-shirt intent on getting rid of it, but I can't resist the urge to touch her skin. I splay my hands on her stomach and she heaves in a breath.

"Your skin is as soft as silk. I want to touch it constantly." I watch my hands dance over her stomach.

"Who's stopping you?"

I chuckle. "You."

"Not anymore."

My heart skips a beat at her answer. Does she mean it? Is she willing to give a relationship with me a chance? Or is this sex talk?

I'm not willing to delve into a discussion about the future right now. Not when I have her panting for me.

"This needs to go," I say before dragging her t-shirt up and over her head. I don't let the garment fall to the floor. Instead, I use it to tie her hands behind her back.

"On your knees."

I gently press on her shoulders but she doesn't need any prodding from me. She sinks to the floor. When she gazes up at me, I have to grit my teeth before I come at the sight of her.

Her breasts are nearly spilling out of her bra with her heaving breath, she's flushed from her face down to the top of her chest, and her eyes are sparkling with challenge. Fuck yeah.

I pop the button of my jeans before drawing down the zipper. My cock strains against my underwear and I pull it out. I tug it a few times before sitting on the edge of the bed.

Soleil crawls closer until I can feel her breath on me. She stares up at me and lifts an eyebrow. Good girl. Waiting for direction from me. Fucking perfect.

"Go ahead, pixie. Put your lips on me."

I use my hand on her chin to guide her mouth to my cock. She gazes up at me as she licks around the head. I groan. One simple lick and I'm already a goner.

I fist her hair. "Don't toy with me."

Her eyes sparkle as she opens her mouth and takes me inside. My head drops back as I moan at the feeling of her hot, wet mouth surrounding me. Nothing has ever felt better. Nothing.

She swallows and the back of her throat tightens around me. I grit my teeth before I come. I am not coming after two licks like some damn teenager.

Her head lifts and she swirls her tongue around my tip a few times before diving in again. She sucks hard as she takes as much of me inside her as she can. Holy hell! Where did she learn to do this?

Nope. I force those thoughts out of my mind. Other men are immaterial. I will be the only man she places her mouth on from here on out.

My balls tingle to let me know I don't have long. I tighten my hold on Soleil's hair. "If you don't want me to come down your throat, stop."

She pauses for a moment and disappointment rolls through me. But then she gazes up at me with a twinkle in her eye before swallowing around my cock. It's all I need to go off.

"Soleil," I growl as my orgasm rips through me.

I can't stop myself from pumping my hips. She swallows everything I give her without complaint. When I'm spent, I pull myself away and she drops back to sit on her heels.

"Are you trying to kill me?"

She giggles. "Oh, please. Dying during sex is probably on your bucket list."

"Not until I've done all the things I've fantasized about doing to you."

"What things?"

"I can't tell you. I have to show you."

"What are you waiting for?"

"Are you challenging me?"

She shrugs. "Maybe."

I haul her onto the bed on top of me. "First, a kiss."

I meld my lips to hers. She sighs and I press my tongue inside. She tastes of honey with a hint of salt. I know I'm tasting myself but I don't care. The taste is a combination of the two of us, which turns me on.

I feel myself lengthen and harden as she squirms on top of me. She gasps and lifts her mouth.

"Are you ready to go again?"

"Not quite, but I will be soon."

"I guess there's an advantage to being with a younger man after all."

"Oh, pixie, my cock isn't eager for another round because I'm younger. He's eager because it's you."

I untie her hands before flipping us, so I'm on top. She reaches for me, but I shake my head.

"Not yet."

"No fair," she pouts.

She won't be pouting long if I have anything to say about it. I yank the cups of her bra down before latching onto her nipple. She arches her back shoving her breasts into my face. Fine by me. I tease one nipple with my teeth while I knead the other breast.

I inch away. "Still think it's not fair?"

She looks at me with glossy eyes. "What's not fair?"

I chuckle as I lay her back on the bed before dragging her bra down her arms.

"Hold onto the headboard."

I wait until she latches onto the headboard before using the bra to secure her hands.

I kiss her nose. "You with me?"

"Uh-huh."

Shit. Condoms. I jump off the bed.

"Where are you going?"

"Need to grab a condom. I won't enter you bear again until I have my test results back."

Call me an optimist but I went to White Bridge to get tested the day after we had sex the first time.

She indicates the nightstand. "Top drawer."

I open the drawer and grin when I notice what else is in the drawer. I pull out the vibrator. "Well. Well. Well. What do we have here?"

She rolls her eyes. "I hope I don't need to explain."

I drop the vibrator back in the drawer and grab a condom from the box. "We'll play with that another time."

I shove my pants down my legs and don the condom before returning to the bed. The sight nearly undoes me. Soleil – the woman of my dreams – is topless and tied to the bed. Her nipples are hard peaks my fingers itch to play with more. But first, those pants need to go.

I unzip her jeans before drawing them down her legs. Soleil may be short but her legs are long and shapely. I throw the jeans over my shoulder before climbing onto the bed.

I glide my hands along her legs as I settle my hips between her thighs. "Love your skin, pixie."

"All natural honey products." I laugh at her answer.

"Are you ready for me?" I ask as I tease her opening with my fingers. Her excitement leaks from her. "Did sucking me off excite you?"

"Yes," she sighs as I plunge two fingers into her.

"Does this excite you?" I ask as I pump my fingers in and out of her.

"Yes," she moans.

"You ready for more?"

"Yes."

I guide my cock to her entrance. "Hold tight to the head-board, pixie girl. This is going to be quick and dirty."

I wait until her hands tighten around the slats before thrusting into her. I pause when I'm buried to the hilt. I thought I was imagining how good it felt the first time I was inside her. I was wrong. It does feel as good as I remember. Maybe better.

I pump in and out of her a few times before getting to my knees. I throw her ankles over my shoulders and she moans.

"You good?"

"Yes," she breathes out.

"Good because I love how deep I can get with your ankles wrapped around my ears."

I sink into her again. Further than before. And have to stop myself before I climax. I'm not coming again until Soleil does.

I pump in and out of her a few times before slinking my hand between us and finding her clit. The second I touch the plump button, she groans and arches her back.

"Are you going to come for me?" I ask as I work her clit while thrusting in and out of her.

She grunts.

"I didn't hear you." I pinch her clit and she cries out.

"I need you to come," I growl as I begin to pound into her. Her eyes dilate and her breath hitches. "Now!"

"Brody!" she shouts as her inner muscles clamp down on me.

I couldn't stop my orgasm now if I wanted to. And I don't want to.

"Soleil!"

I continue to pump into her until I'm completely depleted and she sags into the mattress. Once I recover my breath, I untie her and rub her wrists a bit.

"Need to deal with the condom." I kiss her nose before slowly withdrawing from her and rolling off the bed.

By the time I return, she's asleep. Good. She needs her sleep. I crawl into bed and gather her near. Tomorrow will be another fight about where this relationship is going. In the meantime, I'm going to enjoy her being in my arms.

Chapter 24

"GOOD MORNING, PIXIE."

Brody places a kiss on my neck and draws me closer to him. I snuggle deep into his body. I want to wake up this way every morning.

Too bad waking up with him every morning is a dream. I can't be with someone who's younger than me. Someone who thinks making a person shit their pants is hilarious. Someone whose maturity level is even younger than his actual age. Some-one who reminds me of my dad.

I want someone to take care of *me*.

Except Brody has taken care of me. For the past week, he's cooked every night. He also cleaned the house without me telling him to. And he makes me see stars when we're in bed.

Damn. Is Brody the man I'm searching for? The one who won't expect me to do everything for him? Am I – gulp – falling for him?

He nibbles on my ear. "What has you thinking so hard this early in the morning?"

I clear my throat. I don't know where to begin.

He squeezes my hip. "It's okay. I know this was a one night thing."

"It was?"

"The bed for the spare bedroom should be arriving today. I'm going to pick it up in White Bridge."

I roll to face him.

"Why are you going to White Bridge to pick up the bed?"

He chuckles. "When I phoned the furniture company to ask why the bed hadn't been delivered, they said I rang to delay the delivery."

My brow furrows. "You did?"

He tweaks my nose. "Nope. And I'm not an elderly woman either." He must notice the confusion on my face because he explains. "When I asked who rang to delay the delivery, they said my grandmother did."

I groan. "The gossip gals strike again."

"Exactly. Which is why I'm having the bed delivered to a friend's house in White Bridge where I'll pick it up. I figure the gossip gals won't be able to thwart the delivery this way."

I fiddle with his chest hair. "What if you didn't have the bed delivered?"

His body freezes. Oh no. Has he changed his mind about me? Am I making a mistake?

"Never mind. Forget I said anything."

He grasps my chin and tilts my head up. "I'm not forgetting anything you say. What do you mean? Not have the bed delivered?"

"What if there's no reason for you to sleep in the spare bedroom?"

"I'm not sleeping on the couch any longer than I have to. I still have the scar from when I fell. Plus, my brothers figured it out and now I'll never hear the end of it."

"There's another place in the house you could sleep."

"Soleil Hawk, are you messing with me?"

"I would never mess with you."

He frowns. "Such a shame since I want to mess with you all the time. Get you all messy and dirty."

I squirm at the image his words create. I want to be dirty with him as often as possible. I slink my hand down his chest but he captures my wrist.

"Nuh-uh. No getting dirty until you explain what you meant."

"What I meant?" What were we talking about again? Were we not discussing getting down and dirty?

He palms my cheek with his free hand. "Are you serious? Do you want me to sleep in the same bed with you every night?"

"Who said anything about sleep?"

"Now you're teasing me."

"You tease me all the time."

His eyes warm. "Because you love it."

I can't deny it. I do. I love how he takes charge of giving pleasure in the bedroom. I don't have to do anything but lay back and enjoy myself. It's freeing and exciting and everything I never knew I wanted.

I feign indifference. "Meh. Maybe."

"I'll show you how much you love me teasing you," he growls.

Goodie! I am one hundred percent on board with this plan. Starting now. I dance the fingertips of my free hand over his chest and he moans.

"You're killing me."

He snatches my hand.

"My hands appear tiny next to yours."

"There's a reason I nicknamed you my pixie." He kisses my nose. "Stop stalling."

"I'm not stalling."

He cocks an eyebrow. Okay, fine. Maybe I'm stalling a little bit. But this is a big deal for me. I'm beating back all my fears about being with a younger man to ask Brody to sleep in my bed. I might be making the biggest mistake of my life. I'm probably buying a one-way ticket to the heartbreak hotel. And I've heard the hotel has bed bugs.

"You don't need to pick up the bed because you can sleep with me," I say as fast as I can.

"Sleep with you with a Soleil Wall between us?"

"No walls."

He maneuvers us until he's looming over me. "Will I be your dirty little secret?"

"You can't keep a secret in Winter Falls."

"Maybe you can."

My nose wrinkles. "What do you mean? Are you keeping secrets?"

"Nope."

His answer came way too fast. He's definitely keeping a secret.

I open my mouth to grill him about his secret but snap it shut again when I realize I'm keeping secrets from him, too. He doesn't know how jealous I am of my friends and their families. How I'm dying to have children of my own. A whole bunch of children running around the house causing havoc.

And I'm not telling him. I don't know where this thing with Brody will go. But I do know if I unload my dreams of being a mother on him, he'll suddenly be able to find somewhere else in Winter Falls to live. I don't want him living anywhere else than with me.

Whoa! *Slow down, Soleil.* Brody and I are barely in a relationship. We're not living together, living together.

Brody taps my nose. "Where did you go? And do they have unicorns that fart jellybeans there?"

"Jellybeans?"

He shrugs. "I'm a sucker for cinnamon jellybeans."

"Cinnamon is the best flavor. Have you tried—" He places a finger over my lips to quiet me.

"Soleil Hawk, do you want to be in a relationship with me? One the entire town of Winter Falls knows about. One the entire town will make bets about. They'll probably spy on us, too."

My heart hammers in my chest as fear grips me. Am I making a mistake? Will I regret it? Is Brody too immature for me? There's only one way to find out. Put on my big girl panties and say yes.

"Yes."

His smile stretches from ear to ear. "There's my girl."

"No pranking me during our relationship."

"But pranking is my love language," he pouts.

"Is it love when you trick your brother into thinking he has a broken leg?"

"Yep. It's brotherly love."

"You're incorrigible."

"And I'm all yours."

The butterflies in my stomach awaken. They don't bother stretching their wings. They immediately take off flying. They ram into my stomach as if they're trying to escape their cage. I place a hand on my middle and order them to calm down.

"But I'm still going to pick up the bed today."

"What?"

He draws a finger down my cheek. "I don't want you to feel obligated to sleep in the same bed as me. Not when we're this new. I want you to have the option of kicking me out knowing I won't be sleeping on the couch or the floor."

"Okay," I give in since I don't want him sleeping on the couch or floor ever again.

"Anything else we need to discuss?"

"I don't think so."

"Good," he murmurs before his lips crash down on mine. His tongue traces my mouth before he pushes for entry. I don't deny him. I'm not an idiot after all.

Beep! Beep! Beep!

Crap. My alarm. I yank away from Brody and reach for my phone to switch it off. I check the time and swear under my breath.

"I need to get going."

Brody flops to his back on the bed with a groan. "My first day as a boyfriend and I'm cut off from sex already."

I wag my finger at him. "Keep complaining and I won't let you join me in the shower."

He knifes up and jumps off the bed. "Come on," he tags my hand and leads me to the bathroom. "Let me show you how awesome I am at shower sex."

"I need to leave in thirty minutes."

He smirks. "Challenge accepted."

Oh goodie.

Chapter 25

Brody squeezes my hand as we walk toward the entrance of the Winter Falls' library. "There's no reason to be nervous."

"I'm not nervous," I lie.

"We're just your average couple going on a date."

I snort. "To movie night in a small town where everyone knows our business."

Since Winter Falls is too small to have a movie theater, we have movie night once a month in the library. Ashlyn's sister, Juniper, is in charge of the movies since she's married to Maverick Langston.

Yes, *the* Maverick Langston. The movie star. To those of us in town, he's just plain old Maverick. The man who chased Juniper around until she gave in to him. They're married now, so he must have done something right.

Brody waggles his eyebrows. "They don't know everything."

I like the way he's thinking. "We can go back home and explore what 'everything' can be all by ourselves."

He chuckles. "Nice try. Not happening. My girl and I are going out on a date." He leans close to whisper in my ear. "And then, afterward, I'll explore every inch of her until she screams my name in ecstasy."

I fan my face. "I like this idea. I approve of this idea."

"What idea?" Ashlyn asks as she pops up in front of us. I'd ask where she came from, but it would be a waste of breath. Ashlyn prides herself on being sneaky.

"None of your business."

She rubs her hands together. "Awesome. Those are the best ideas."

I push past her. I'm not in the mood for her craziness today. I open the door to the library and everyone swivels toward it to see who's arriving. Quiet falls for a few moments before everyone starts talking at once as soon as they realize who just arrived. And I'm pretty sure I see money exchange hands. This town and betting. Maybe I should have stuck with Ashlyn's craziness after all.

I cling to Brody's hand. "Let's go find a seat."

I drag him toward the rear of the room but I don't make it far before Juniper steps in front of me. "You're going the wrong way."

"There's not a seating chart."

She snorts. "You're cute. Now, go." She points to the front of the room.

"What is she talking about?" Brody asks.

"This isn't necessary." I lift up our joined hands. "We're already dating."

"It's not official."

It felt pretty damn official when he went to his knees in the shower this morning.

Juniper crosses her arms over her chest. "I don't make the rules."

"Sure, you don't," I mutter before twirling around and stomping toward the front of the room. I run into Sage and the gossip gals halfway there.

I wag my finger at Sage. "You're on my shit list."

She grasps her chest and widens her eyes. "Me? Whatever did I do?"

"Save your innocent act. You haven't been innocent since the Carter administration."

She fists her hands on her hips. "Watch what you say, little missy. I changed your diapers."

I ignore the diaper comment. I still haven't figured out why changing my diapers as a baby should hold power over me.

"You watch it. No more messing with bed deliveries."

She grins. "You have to admit having only one bed worked out well for you."

Brody taps his temple. "Except for my battle injury."

Sage's eyes twinkle. "Too bad no one else in Winter Falls had any room for Brody to stay with them."

I gasp. "You cheater!"

"All's fair in love and war," she sings before wandering off with the gossip gals following her.

"Hey!" I shout after her. "You didn't promise to stop messing with us."

"What did you say? This old lady can't hear very well any-more."

Liar. She can hear better than most young people. Brody wraps an arm around my shoulders. I can feel him shaking with laughter. I try to push him off of me. "It's not funny."

"Come on. An eighty-year-old bested you. It's hilarious."

"She didn't best me."

"Okay."

I elbow him. "You're still laughing."

We make our way to the loveseat in the front of the room. It's the loveseat all newly minted couples have to sit on at movie night. I don't know how the tradition started but I will see an end to it.

I flop down and Brody hands me a tub of popcorn. The smell of caramel wafts toward me.

"Where did you get the caramel corn?"

"I ordered ahead since I know it's your favorite."

"How do you know it's my favorite?"

"Because I pay attention, pixie." He tweaks my nose. "Now, what do you want to drink? I have orange soda, water, beer, and wine."

"When did you manage all this?"

"I'm a man of mystery."

"Okay, man of mystery. Do you have any candy?"

"Of course. I have cinnamon gummy bears, cinnamon gum drops, and cinnamon jellybeans."

"No chocolate?"

"Nice try. I know cinnamon is your favorite."

"You're annoying."

"I'm annoying because I know you prefer cinnamon over chocolate?"

"You know what I mean," I grumble before holding out my hand. "Water please."

The lights flicker before Juniper walks to the front of the room. "Ahem." She clears her throat when the noise doesn't quiet down. "Ahem!"

When no one shuts up, she shouts, "Who wants to know what tonight's movie is?"

"I already know," Ashlyn shouts back.

"Fifty bucks says you don't," Juniper snaps.

"I'm with Ashlyn," Moon says.

Juniper rolls her eyes. "Naturally. You two are inseparable. I'm surprised you're not sister wives."

"Why sister wives? Why not brother husbands? Why does the woman have to share the man? Why can't I have two men instead?" Ashlyn asks. Her husband growls and she pats his chest. "I don't need two men. I have Rowan, but it's the principal of the thing."

"I'm not being prejudiced against women. I'm merely pointing out how you and Moon are inseparable."

Riley stands. "I volunteer as tribute."

Moon elbows him. "I'm not sharing you with Ashlyn."

He waggles his eyebrows at her. "But I'm loveable and there's plenty of me to go around."

"Ew. And I think the word you're searching for is annoying."

"Annoyingly loveable."

I munch on my popcorn as I watch the show. This is better than any movie.

Moon glares at Riley. "Annoying and loveable do not belong in the same sentence."

He smirks. "They do if it's me."

Juniper claps her hands. "Can we start the movie now?"

"My fifty bucks says the movie is *The Rebound*," Ashlyn claims.

Juniper glares at her. "How did you know? Did you sneak into my house again? I fixed the bathroom window."

"Which is super annoying by the way. The doggy door is a tight fit." Ashlyn shivers.

"I guess I'll be adopting a replacement for Slinky."

"Ha! You don't scare me. You wouldn't dare. I know Maverick hates snakes as much as I do."

Juniper grins. "Maverick's away shooting a film now."

Ashlyn waves her phone. "He's merely a press of a button away."

Brody kisses my hair. "Aren't you glad you didn't chicken out and stay at home?"

"I wasn't close to chickening out," I claim. "Now. Shush. This is good entertainment."

He licks the shell of my ear. "I can provide good entertainment." His hand sneaks under my tub of popcorn but I bat him away.

"Behave."

"Why? Behaving is boring. Being bad has way more rewards." He traces his fingers along the skin above the waistband of my jeans.

"What about patience being a virtue?"

"I'm more an instant satisfaction kind of guy."

I snort. "No, you're not, Mr. Tease."

"Mr. Tease? Perfect. I'll allow you to use this moniker when referring to me."

"You'll allow me? You're delusional. How much beer have you had to drink?"

"I haven't had—"

Juniper's clapping cuts him off. "Brody. Soleil. Can you pay attention with the rest of the class?"

My nose scrunches in feigned distaste. "Is this a class?"

"Will there be a test at the end? Should I be taking notes?" Brody asks.

She spears a glare at us before returning her attention to Ashlyn. "How did you know what movie I'd chosen this month?"

Ashlyn snorts. "There aren't a whole ton of reverse age gap movies out there."

I groan. Of course, tonight's movie is a reverse age gap. Way to remind me I'm too old for Brody and we shouldn't be pursuing a relationship. Way to remind me I'm repeating my mom's mistake – pursuing a relationship with a younger man.

"I love reverse age gap," Feather says. "We should read a reverse age gap in smutty book club."

"We read a reverse age gap last month," Petal reminds her.

"We can read another one. The scenes are hot, hot, hot."

"An older woman training a younger man to be perfect for him? I'm in," Clove says.

"My dearly departed Arlo was ten years younger than me. I wouldn't have had it any other way." Cayenne sighs.

Hold on a sec. They're not reminding me I'm too old for Brody. They're trying to show me it's okay if I'm older and he's younger.

Of course, they're the gossip gals. They want to matchmake everyone. Although, they don't match any two random people together. They try to create solid matches. Matches that will stand the test of time.

Huh. Am I making too big a deal of the age gap between Brody and me?

Brody isn't my dad, after all.

Chapter 26

RILEY: DID EVERYONE NOTICE Brody staring at Soleil with cartoon hearts in his eyes last night?

Damon: No. I don't live in Winter Falls. Or did you forget?

Brody: Yeah, Riley. Are you having memory problems?

Riley: Nope. I remember exactly how you tripped over your feet to get Soleil's attention last night.

Brody: I didn't trip over my feet. Pretty sure you were the one getting in trouble with Moon for suggesting you want to be in a throuple with her best friend.

Damon: Hold on. Riley's in a throuple?

Elder: You'd know if you lived in Winter Falls.

Brody: Yeah, Damon. Why don't you live in Winter Falls?

Damon: None of your business.

Elder: Damon's hiding a secret! Damon's hiding a secret!

Riley: Nope. It's Brody time. Not Damon time.

Brody: Is this like Miller time? Are we going to drink beer in the sand bunker of a golf course and make fun of the golfers and their hats like in those old tv commercials?

Riley: *Gasp* Don't let the people of Winter Falls hear you talking about golf. Golf courses are bad for the environment.

Brody: Someone's been indoctrinated.

Riley: I think you mean seen the light.

Elder: Is that what we're calling it nowadays?

Peace: Can we get back to the matter at hand? Some of us have jobs.

Miller: True.

Brody: What's the matter at hand? How Riley is whipped? Pa-chang!

Riley: You wish you were whipped.

Brody: Nope. I do the whipping. Not the other way around.

Peace: Ew. I do not need to hear about what Brody gets up to in the bedroom.

Miller: Agree.

Riley: Brody's telling tall tales anyway.

Brody: Sure. Let's pretend you know the truth.

Damon: Who's Soleil again?

Riley: Brody's sugar mamma.

Brody: Hey! What about twin powers? You're supposed to support me against the rest of these yahoos.

Riley: Twin powers don't apply when we're discussing your sugar mamma.

Brody: I don't have a sugar mama.

Elder: What do you call an older woman whose house you live in and whose bed you sleep in?

Brody: If you say sugar mama, I'm putting a bug on your phone.

Elder: Oh no! I'm soooo scared. Brody's going to make my phone quack like a duck when it rings. Someone save me!

Brody: Quack like a duck is for amateurs. I was thinking more scream bloody murder.

Elder: You wouldn't.

Brody: I'll make sure to call you when you're delivering beer.

Elder: You're an asshole.

Brody: I prefer the word talented but I understand you're jealous and lashing out at me.

Elder: Why the hell would I be jealous of you?

Brody: See the aforementioned talent.

Riley: Aforementioned? When did Brody learn big words?

Damon: I can still remember when he called me Amon after the Egyptian god.

Brody: I called you Amon because I couldn't pronounce the D, not because I thought you were a god, asshole.

Damon: Aw. Did we hurt little baby Brody's feelings?

Brody: I've had it. I'm infecting all of your phones with bugs.

Peace: If my phone quacks like a duck when I'm arresting someone, I'm telling Soleil you wet the bed until you were ten.

Brody: I didn't wet the bed until I was ten.

Elder: It doesn't matter anyway. The only person Peace has arrested lately is Brody.

Brody: He didn't arrest me.

Peace: I did, too. Or do I need to show you your criminal record?

Brody: Please do. I'd love to see it.

Peace: Tell me you didn't hack into the Winter Falls police records.

Brody: I didn't hack into the Winter Falls police records.

Peace: Not okay, Brody. Hacking into police records is against several federal laws.

Brody: Which is why I didn't hack into the police records.

Miller: Why are we having this insane conversation? Brody does what Brody does.

Brody: Thanks, bro.

Miller: It wasn't a compliment.

Brody: You say potato, I say tomato. Potato. Tomato. Potato. Tomato.

Riley: Can we return to how Brody has a sugar mama now?

Damon: Who is this Soleil? Do we approve of her?

Elder: We approve of her. The jury's still out on him.

Brody: Ha! Ha! You're so funny.

Elder: I am funny. Speaking of golfing…

Brody: We weren't speaking of golfing.

Elder: Why do dads take an extra pair of socks when they go golfing? In case they get a hole in one! Get it? Hole in one.

Damon: If you have to explain the joke, it's not funny.

Miller: Agree.

Brody: This has been fun but I need to get back to work.

Elder: Work? Piling sketches of medieval weapons on the dining room table isn't work.

Brody: I work. I even have an office in the community center now.

Peace: An office in the community center? The community center is supposed to be for community activities.

Brody: Which can't happen without funding. Which is why they were happy to rent me space.

Elder: Where did you find the money?

Brody: I have money.

Elder: If you have money, why were you mooching off of me?

Riley: And now he's mooching off of Soleil.

Damon: He has the trust fund money from Dad, remember?

Brody: I'm not using my trust fund money.

Damon: Then what money are you using?

Peace: You better not be stealing money from people's bank accounts.

Brody: Where the hell would you get such an idea? I'm not a thief.

Peace: And you didn't try to break into the library.

Brody: This conversation is dumb. I have things to do.

Riley: How's the shed construction coming?

Damon: Hold on. Catch me up. Brody is building a shed? Brody who thinks pliers are for removing toenails?

Brody: I was five!

Elder: He's trying to impress his sugar mamma by replacing her pottery shed that burned down.

Brody: Soleil is not my sugar mamma!

Riley: He downloaded plans from the internet and is now convinced he's Bob the Builder. It's actually quite cute.

Brody: I'm a man. I'm handsome, not cute.

Miller: You keep telling yourself that.

Peace: I keep my radio on 24/7 so I won't miss the call when he accidentally cuts off his foot.

Brody: Statistically, I'm more likely to cut off a finger than my foot.

Peace: Good to know. A finger is easier to replace.

Damon: I need to visit Winter Falls.

Brody: You should move here.

Damon: I have a life in San Diego.

Brody: A life that includes a significant other?

Damon: Gotta go.

Damon has left the conversation.

Miller: I'm out of here.

Brody: Work is calling.

Riley: What work????

Chapter 27

Has anyone seen my golf cart? ~ Message from Miller on the Winter Falls Facebook page

"HELLO," I ANSWER THE phone as I walk into the house.

The last thing I want to do after a long day of throwing pots is talk on the phone. But this call is from the insurance company. The insurance company I need to pay me before I can start building a new shed.

I can't continue to work at the community center much longer. Everyone in town thinks it's okay to come by for a chat. I don't have time for chatting. Especially when I know the real reason, they're 'checking on me', is to prod for information about me and Brody in order to win the Project Cub bet.

"This is Donna from Alpha Delta Omega Insurance Company."

I don't bother with pleasantries. "When can I expect the insurance money?"

"Ms. Hawk, I'm afraid we won't be paying out for a while."

I come to a halt in the entryway. "What?"

"We won't be paying out for a while," she repeats.

"Yes, I heard you. What I want to know is why? I've paid my premiums every single month for over ten years. I don't understand why there's any delay."

Brody arrives and lifts my bag off my shoulder before grasping my elbow and guiding me to the living room. I settle on the sofa and he sits next to me. He wraps his arm around my shoulders and I lean into him. Thankful for his support.

"According to the investigation, your kiln had an electric short which caused the fire."

"You can't blame me for a problem with the kiln I didn't know about."

"Alpha Delta Omega has a different view of this."

"Different view? What do you mean?"

"It means that if you weren't diligent when you purchased the kiln, then we won't honor your claim."

"You didn't have a problem accepting my monthly payments for a decade."

"Yes, well, there's nothing I can do about it. I'm merely the messenger."

I inhale a deep breath. She's right. There's no sense in being frustrated with her. She doesn't have any power here. "Is there anyone I can speak to who does have an influence on the outcome of my case?"

"I'm afraid a manager isn't available at this time."

"If you can provide me with a name and number, I'll call back."

"I'm afraid I'm not allowed to provide you with that information."

"This is ridiculous. I'm seriously reconsidering using your company for any future insurance needs I may have."

"You're free to choose whichever insurance provider you desire, Ms. Hawk. If there's nothing else, have a good day." She hangs up before I have a chance to tell her whether there's anything else or not.

I throw the phone on the coffee table before burying my face in my hands and groaning. "This is a disaster."

Brody rubs circles on my back. "What's a disaster? What's happening?"

"The insurance company is stalling on paying me," I mumble into my hands.

Brody pulls my hands away and palms my neck to draw my face near to his. "Again?"

"The insurance company is stalling."

"I'm sorry, pixie." He brushes my hair off my forehead before planting a kiss there. "But at least you can work at the community center in the meantime."

"The kiln at the community center is too small for long-term use, which is why I donated it to the center in the first place."

He massages my neck. "I understand, but it's better than nothing, isn't it?"

"I'm way behind on my orders."

"I'm sure your customers understand. It's not as if they're buying from some big faceless mega-store. They're buying art from an artist."

Actually, he's right. Most of my customers have been very understanding. I prioritized the few who weren't and got their pieces finished ahead of the line.

"And you can let new customers know there's a long wait. Don't long waits for art make it more special?"

I roll my eyes. "I think you're going overboard on the art stuff."

"I've seen your pottery. It's art."

My stomach warms at his words of approval. My mom always supported my art but Dad still refers to it as artsy fartsy. Merely one of the many reasons we barely speak anymore.

Lucky for me, he moved back to his hometown after Mom died. I wouldn't get away with giving him the cold shoulder if he lived in town. Sage wouldn't allow it.

"You think my pottery is art?" I'm not begging for compliments. Okay, I am. But I want to hear him say my work is art again.

"Pixie, your pottery is more than art. It's amazing."

"Thank you."

His lips touch mine in a brief kiss before he stands and offers me his hand. "Come on. Time to go."

"Go where?" I wag my eyebrows. "The bedroom?"

"The bedroom's for later tonight." He winks. "For now, I have a surprise for you."

I grasp his hand and he draws me to his feet. "A surprise? What kind of surprise?"

"Something to make you forget all about the insurance company."

I snort. "That's a tall order."

He bows. "I live to serve."

"Dork."

"Your dork." He kisses my nose and leads me out of the house.

"Where are we going?"

"It wouldn't be a surprise if I told you, now would it?"

We walk to the end of the street before turning toward Main Street. "A walk is nice."

"It is but an evening stroll isn't your surprise."

When we reach Main Street, I notice a crowd gathered on the sidewalk.

"What's going on? All the shops are closed. Why are people milling about?"

He waves toward two golf carts parked in the middle of the street in front of the pet store, *Unleashed.* "For this."

I'm confused. There are always plenty of golf carts in Winter Falls. It is the main mode of transportation after all.

"What's happening?"

He grins. "It's a race!"

"A race?"

"Yep. You and I are going to race down Main Street to *Electric Vibes.* The loser has to buy a round for everyone at the bar."

"Now I understand why everyone in town is here."

He cups my face. "What's wrong? Are you afraid to lose?"

"Afraid to lose?" I scoff.

"I am the reigning Winter Falls golf cart race champion."

"There isn't such a thing."

He winks. "There is now."

"Is this even legal?"

He points to Peace. "The fuzz is here and they're not arresting us."

"Yet. He's not arresting us *yet*."

"Peace!" Brody shouts. "Are you going to arrest us if we race these golf carts down Main Street?"

Peace strolls over. "Here are the rules."

"You didn't say anything about rules earlier," Brody pouts.

"Yes, I did. I can't help it if you didn't listen." Brody rolls his eyes and Peace continues, "You have fifteen minutes to perform this race. After fifteen minutes, I'll be arresting anyone still in a golf cart."

Brody rubs his hands together. "No problem. I'll be on my second drink by then."

"No tequila!" Peace yells.

Brody frowns. "As if I can buy tequila in this town."

I have no idea what they're talking about. "What are the other rules?" I ask Peace.

"Stay on Main Street. No going over sidewalks or using the alleys and definitely no driving over the town square."

"Okay. Anything else?"

"You have to wear a helmet and gloves."

"A helmet and gloves?" I ask. "The top speed of a golf cart is fifteen miles per hour."

"Those are the rules," Peace says. "Accept them or don't race."

"I don't have a helmet or gloves."

Brody catches my hand. "I got you covered."

"I guess I accept the rules then."

Peace grunts before leaving. His girlfriend, Olivia, moves to stand in the center of the road. "I'm the starter." She removes a red bra from her sleeve and waves it in the air.

Peace growls. "Olivia!"

She bats her eyelashes at him. "What? I'm not braless. I wasn't wearing this bra. It's merely a prop."

Brody ushers me to one of the golf carts. On the seat is a bright pink helmet with the word 'Pixie' in gold letters on it. He lifts the helmet and places it on my head before buckling the strap. "You good?"

I wiggle my hands. "I need gloves."

He chuckles as he picks the pink gloves up from the seat and hands them to me. He kisses my cheek before moving to his golf cart and putting on a black helmet with the word 'Dork' engraved on it.

"Are the riders ready?" Olivia shouts the question while lifting her red bra in the air.

I situate myself in the cart and switch it on while Brody revs his engine.

"Ready, set, ride!" Olivia throws her bra onto the ground and I slam the accelerator down to the floor.

The crowd cheers as we pass them. It's less than a mile before we reach *Electric Vibes*. I don't have much time to win this race, but I'm determined to beat Brody.

"I'm winning! I'm winning!" Brody shouts as he pulls into the lead.

We're barreling straight toward the town square. If I can force him onto the square, he'll be disqualified and I'll win. Mwah-ha-ha!

I keep up with him until we reach *Clove's Coffee Corner,* which is the last business before the square. Since I'm on the right side, it would make sense for me to veer to the right to go around the square. I veer left instead and cut Brody off.

"Hey! You're cheating," he yells as he tries to keep control of his golf cart.

"Nobody said I couldn't cheat," I yell back.

"You're in trouble now," he says as he chases me around the left side of the square past the library and toward Eden's plant shop.

"I'll believe it when I see it."

Unfortunately, it isn't long before we're back on the straight of Main Street racing next to each other. Shit. *Electric Vibes* is only five stores away. I have to do something or I'll lose this race. And I am not losing.

I swerve to the right toward Brody's golf cart. He swears as he maneuvers out of range. He's crazy if he thinks I'm done. This race is officially bumper golf cart now.

I aim straight for his golf cart. He has no choice. He either has to let me hit him or swerve onto the sidewalk.

He swears as he swerves and ends up on the sidewalk in front of the community center.

"Whoo hoo!" I throw my hands in the air as I pass the finish line in front of the bar. "I'm the winner."

Brody jumps out of his golf cart and stalks toward me. "You're a cheater is what you are."

"Peace didn't say anything about not hitting the other golf cart in his list of rules."

"Sneaky." He grins. "I like it."

He reaches me and shackles my wrist to drag me out of my golf cart. His gaze focuses on my lips and I lick them. His head descends and bang! Our helmets collide.

He chuckles. "I forgot about the helmets."

"I noticed." I smile. "Thanks for cheering me up."

"You don't need to thank me. It's my privilege and pleasure to make a bad day into a good day for you."

"You say the sweetest things."

His chest puffs up. "I know. I am pretty awesome."

I slap him. "Dork."

"Sexy dork who you can't wait to drag you home and ravage you."

I open my mouth to correct him but shrug when I realize he's right. "Let's go home."

Home. I love the idea of having a home with this man. I stumble when I realize why. I'm falling in love with him. Oh boy. I hope I didn't just take the exit from the highway for the Heartbreak Hotel.

Chapter 28

Can I call in sick to family dinner night? ~ Text from Soleil to Eden

I TUG ON BRODY's hand before we can turn into the walkway leading to Peace's mom's house.

"I don't know if this is a good idea."

His brow furrows. "Why not? It's family dinner night."

"Exactly. It's *family* dinner night."
He scratches his neck. "I'm confused."

I narrow my eyes on him. He's not confused. He's being obtuse. On purpose. "I'm not part of your family."

"You're my girlfriend."

"Of two weeks," I remind him.

"One," he begins and I sigh. He only counts off reasons when he's being stubborn. "Time is immaterial. You and me together feels good. Feels right. Who cares if it's been two weeks or two months or two years or two decades?"

My insides go all squishy at his words. Damn him. Being all sweet again.

"And, two, a girlfriend is a member of the family."

"Except my twin has never had a girlfriend before," Riley says as he and Moon join us on the sidewalk.

Brody goes after him but Peace appears and steps between them. "Who knew being a police officer would be such good training for being a big brother?"

"I knew," Elder says as he and Harmony stop next to us.

Harmony's holding baby Robin and I immediately reach out my hands. "Gimme."

"If she has an accident while you're holding her, you have to change her," Harmony says as she hands me the baby.

I cuddle Robin close. "You wouldn't have an accident while Auntie Soleil is holding you, would you, baby girl?"

Harmony barks out a laugh. "If she has accidents while Elder, who is her favorite person in the whole world holds her, she'll have an accident whenever she wants."

Elder snatches the baby from my hands. "I am Robin's favorite person."

Harmony sighs. "This is going to be fun when she hits dating age."

"By the time she's twenty-five, she'll understand how men can be dawgs and how she has to force them to respect her."

Olivia walks out of the house and comes to stand next to me. "What are we discussing?"

Harmony points to Elder. "What an idiot my husband is. He thinks he can prevent our daughter from dating until she's twenty-five."

"My house. My rules."

Olivia barks out a laugh. "My brother, Beckett, tried the same thing with me. Didn't work. In fact, it made me want to do the opposite of what he said."

"Because you're a troublemaker," Peace says.

"Are we discussing Moon?" Eden asks as she strolls our way hand in hand with Miller.

Moon beams at her. "No, but thank you for recognizing my troublemaker capabilities."

Riley kisses her nose. "You're the best kind of troublemaker."

Miller glances around the gathering and grunts, "Hungry," before marching toward the house.

"He's always hungry," Eden grumbles as she trails after him.

The rest of the Bragg family follow Miller and Eden but Brody tugs on my hand to stop me.

"Feel better about the family dinner now?"

"I still think it's weird you have a family dinner with the woman who your father cheated on your mother with while they were engaged."

He shrugs. "I can't help it. Clementine adopted us. Besides, Mom's here, too."

I gulp. Daisy's here, too?

He drops my hand to frame my face with his palms. "Relax, Soleil. You know everyone here and they all love you."

I blow out a breath. "I know. I don't know why I'm making a big deal of this."

"I get it. You're scared of your feelings for me." He smirks.

I glare at him. "Full of yourself, aren't you?"

"Nope. But you'll be full of me as soon as we leave dinner."

My breath hitches and my belly warms. Sex with Brody is out of this world. Who knew the prankster became a dominating sex machine in the bedroom?

"Stop whispering sweet nothings in her ear and get in here," Daisy hollers from the front porch.

"I wasn't whispering sweet nothings," Brody returns.

I smack him. "Don't tell your mom what you said."

"Why not? She knows I have sex."

"Oh boy, do I know," Daisy says as we reach her. "You wouldn't believe the amount of water the five of them wasted when they went through puberty. It's a good thing I had a master bathroom or I wouldn't have gotten a chance to shower for a decade."

She laces her arm through mine. "Let me tell you about the time he realized girls and boys weren't biologically the same."

"Mom," Brody whines.

She bats her eyelashes. "What? This is the first time you've brought a girlfriend home since eighth grade. I've got years worth of stories saved up."

My heart clutches in my chest. "The first time he brought a girl home since eighth grade?"

Daisy pats my hand. "Don't worry. He's had girlfriends. Or, at least, hook-ups judging by the number of times women answered his phone when I rang him early in the morning."

"Maybe you should have stopped phoning early in the morning," Brody complains.

"And miss the chance to embarrass you? Why would I do a silly thing like that?"

"Because moms aren't supposed to embarrass their children."

"Now, you're being ridiculous." Daisy drags me further into the house. Her fiancé, Lennon, smiles and walks toward her but she waves him away. He chuckles as he veers off in another direction. Smart man.

"Now, where was I?"

"The time he realized boys and girls were different," I prod because I have got to hear this.

"You know our Brody, always the prankster. When he was in kindergarten, he pulled a girl's shorts down in recess."

"I didn't mean to pull down her panties," Brody clarifies and I shush him.

"He screamed when he saw she didn't have a penis. In fact, he yelled at her, 'Where's your wee-wee? Did you lose it?' And then all hell broke loose because he now thought it was possible for his penis to fall off. The school nurse phoned me and when I arrived, he was still screaming, 'I don't want my wee-wee to fall off!'"

I burst out laughing.

"I'm not finished," Daisy says and I nod for her to continue. "He grabbed a stapler from the nurse and was going to staple his penis to his body."

Daisy and I dissolve into giggles while every man in the room cringes.

Brody crosses his arms over his chest and pouts. "If you had explained the difference between girls and boys to me, none of this would have happened."

"I did explain the difference to you and Riley. It's not my fault you weren't listening."

"You should have made me put down the Legos."

She rolls her eyes. "Have you ever tried to tell a five-year-old to put down their toy and listen to you? It's impossible."

"I'm with Daisy on this," Clementine says as she enters the living room.

"Mom," Peace grumbles at her, "we agreed you would claim I was a model child in front of company."

"What company? Family isn't company."

While Clementine and Peace bicker about his childhood, Brody steals me away from his mom. "Happy you came now?" he whispers into my ear.

"I love your mom."

"Good. Because I plan for you to be around her for a very long time."

"Brody Bragg, don't you dare make declarations about your intentions while we're at dinner with your family," I scold despite how warm and fuzzy his words make me feel. Even my knees are wobbling. Who knew the prankster could do romance?

"It's not an aim or goal. It's what's going to happen."

I cock an eyebrow. "Do I get any say in this?"

"No." I growl and he leans forward to nip my earlobe. "But you do get lots and lots of orgasms."

My panties dampen at his words. I try to push him away. "We're at a family gathering."

Brody doesn't let me push him away. "And? Everyone here knows we're having sex."

My cheeks darken at his words. "It doesn't mean we have to discuss it in front of them."

He runs his nose along mine. "I know discussing sex in front of my family is making you hot for me. You can't deny it when I can see you pressing your legs together."

"You're a jerk."

"Who's hungry?" Peace's dad, Eagle, asks as he carries a platter to the table in the dining area. I want to kiss him for interrupting before I ended up attacking Brody in front of his mom and brothers.

"I'm starving," Miller grumbles as he marches to the table and sits down.

"Such a gentleman," Eden complains as she follows him.

"Why am I not a gentleman?"

"You could have held my chair out for me."

"Why?"

"Is this how it's going to be since we're engaged? Any romance is now a thing of the past?"

I smile at my friend and her happiness. For the first time in a long while my smile isn't forced. I'm truly happy for her and I'm not feeling jealous at all. I glance over at Brody as he holds a chair out for me. It's not hard to figure out the reason why my jealousy has disappeared.

Chapter 29

BRODY

I skid to a halt and shove Soleil behind me when I notice the package on the front porch.

"What are you doing?"

"There's something on the porch."

She snorts. "This is Winter Falls. You can't honestly expect a bomb or anything dangerous. It's probably a cake. Maybe a pineapple upside-down cake."

"Which is dangerous since I'm allergic to pineapple."

"Will you die if you eat it or break out in hives?"

"Does it matter?"

"Well, yeah. One goes into the 'never have it in the house again' column while the other goes into the 'remember this for when he pisses you off' column."

"I won't die but I'll want to as I live through my body trying to force any and all remnants of pineapple out in any way it can."

"Ew. Gross. Too much information."

I shrug. "You asked."

She steps out from behind me but I catch her hand before she can get any closer to the package. "Wait here while I check it out."

She giggles. "You really don't understand the concept of Winter Falls."

"You really don't understand the concept of having five brothers."

"Good point." She motions to the porch. "Please save me, sir. I'm afraid of the basket on the porch."

I tweak her nose. "Your southern accent is atrocious."

"Probably because I was born and raised in Colorado and have barely traveled out of state."

"I'll take you to visit San Diego where I grew up."

"Are you forgetting I have zero free time until my new pottery shed is finished and I can catch up on orders?"

"Nope. But I have faith in you. In it all working out in the end."

"You have faith in me?"

"Why do you appear confused? Of course, I have faith in you. You're my girl."

"I'm not a girl, but I am getting chilly standing out here."

I bow. "I shall save you, fair maiden." I remove my hoodie and hand it to her. "Wait here while I secure our location."

She puts the hoodie on. It hangs nearly to her knees since she's a foot shorter than me. She looks absolutely adorable. I want to eat her up. And I will. But first – the package.

I tiptoe toward the porch. Soleil giggles behind me, but I ignore her. I don't plan to spend the night showering paint off me because I tripped a wire on a prank.

I keep my eyes out for wires as I creep up the stairs. I don't see any and continue toward the package. Which is a basket. Of candles. I pick up the card and jump away before anything can get me but nothing happens.

Soleil is outright laughing at me now. I'll make her pay for laughing at me later.

"Thought you might enjoy these. Signed Petal," I read aloud.

Soleil's laughter cuts off and she moans. "Oh no."

"Oh no, what?" I don't wait for her answer before diving into the basket. It contains a variety of candles. I lift up the black candle. "You up for some wax play?"

I was only kidding but Soleil's breath hitches and her eyes flare. My cock twitches in response. Hell yeah.

I throw the black candle into the basket before lifting it up and grasping Soleil's hand. "Let's go."

"In a hurry?" she asks as I barge into the house.

I don't bother answering as I drag her to the bedroom. I guide her to the bed where she sits down. I place the basket on the bed to dig through it.

"What do we have here?"

I remove a candle from the basket and check to make sure it's body-safe before setting it on the bed. Next is a blindfold. Excellent. Finally, I pull out a set of fuzzy pink handcuffs. I place the items on the bed before setting the basket on the dresser. I'll search through the rest later. I have what I need for now.

I kneel in front of Soleil and grasp her hands. "Are you sure about this?"

A blush stains her cheeks. "I've never done it before. Have you?"

"I have. Do you have questions on how it works?"

"I grew up in Winter Falls with Petal the sex candle maker. I think I know how it works."

I glide my thumbs along her skin. "We don't have to do this. I'm happy to have you any way I can get you."

"But you want to."

"Only if you want to. It's no fun for me if it's not fun for you."

She swallows. "I want to try."

"You're sure?"

"I'm sure. I trust you."

My heart batters in my chest. Soleil – the woman I'm obsessed with – trusts me to give her pleasure.

"I know you would never hurt me."

God. I love her. Whoa. What? I love Soleil? I don't know why the idea is shocking to me. I've been obsessed with the woman for months. And my obsession has only gotten stronger since we've been living together.

I open my mouth to blurt the words out but snap it shut again. Soleil deserves more than a quick 'I love you' before sex. She deserves the whole she-bang – candles, flowers, candy. I'll make it an event.

In the meantime, I surge up to kiss her lips. To taste her honey flavor. To enjoy her warm mouth. I dive in – determined to explore every inch of her mouth before I begin my exploration of the rest of her. I wrap my arms around her waist and slam her body against mine. Her breasts strain against my chest and her hard nipples poke at me.

When my balls begin to tingle, I slow the kiss before drawing my lips across her skin until I can whisper in her ear. "Clothes off. On the bed."

I adjust my cock before I stand and retreat a few steps to allow her to disrobe. She kicks off her sneakers before shoving her jeans down her legs. My sweatshirt is next. She's still removing her t-shirt and bra when she climbs onto the bed.

I chuckle. "Now who's in a hurry?"

She lays down and stretches her arms over her head to grasp the headboard. "Like this?"

Holy fuck. She's a wanton goddess. My wanton goddess. My cock strains against the zipper. I reach down and squeeze the base before I come in my jeans. I am not a damn virgin.

She bites her lips as she watches me. Forget goddess. She's a temptress.

I want to jump on the bed and fuck her senseless but I stop myself. Later. I dig through my stuff to find a lighter and light the candle before going to the bathroom and wetting a washcloth with cold water. I set the washcloth next to the candle. I probably don't need it but I will not risk Soleil's safety.

"The candle wax will melt and become massage oil. Do you want me to put a towel down beneath you for the mess?"

"I have more sheets and know how to do laundry."

I twirl the handcuffs in my fingers. "Are you okay with being handcuffed?"

"Yes."

I lean over her, careful not to touch her, and handcuff her to the headboard. She squirms and rubs her thighs together. I freaking love how turned on this makes her. She's perfect for me.

I set the blindfold next to her hip. "You're not going to blindfold me?" She practically pouts. Yep. Perfect for me.

"I want to see your reaction to the wax before I blindfold you. I don't want you to do this to please me. I want you to do this because you enjoy it."

"Okay."

I lift the candle. "You ready?"

"Y-y-yes." She clears her throat. "Yes."

"I'm going to drip a tiny bit on your thigh first."

I keep my focus on her face as I drip the wax on her thigh. When the hot wax touches her skin, she hisses and bites her lip.

"Okay?"

"Yes," she sighs.

I rub the oil into her skin and goosebumps appear as her eyes fall closed and she moans. Hell yeah. She's not doing this for me. She's enjoying herself.

"Ready for the blindfold?"

She nods. "I need you to say the word."

"Put the blindfold on me, dork."

I chuckle as I place it over her eyes. I make sure it isn't tight before standing and removing my clothes. My cock jumps out and points to Soleil's pussy where he wants to be right now. He'll have to wait. I have some teasing to do first.

I climb back on the bed and position myself on top of Soleil. "If anything I do hurts you or makes you feel uncomfortable, I'll stop immediately."

"Do we need a safe word?"

"We don't but if you want to have one to make you feel more comfortable, we can."

"How about clay?"

"Clay?"

"It's a dirty four letter word."

I chuckle. "Clay it is."

I hold the candle above her stomach. I want to see how sexy she looks with wax dripping all over her breasts, but I need to work up to those sensitive areas.

She squirms. "What are you waiting for?"

"For you to be still."

"Okay. I'll be still."

I wait a minute to make sure she can stay still before pouring a bit of wax on her stomach. She hisses as it hits her skin. Once the wax turns into massage oil, I rub it into her skin and she moans in response.

I continue placing small drops of wax on her stomach on the way to her breasts. Her nipples are already hard but I want them aching for my touch. She presses her thighs together but she doesn't squirm.

"Good girl," I murmur as I place a tiny drop of wax on the underside of her breast and she arches her back to get closer to me. I massage the oil into her skin and she moans as she presses her breast into my hand.

"You're supposed to stay still," I remind her.

"You can't seriously expect me to stay still when you—"

I drip wax onto her other breast and she cuts herself off with a groan. I place the candle on the nightstand. I can't resist the temptation of her breasts any longer. I massage and kneed the soft skin until Soleil is trembling beneath me.

"Is there something you want?"

"I want you."

"I'm right here."

"I want you inside me."

I trail a hand down her stomach past her mound and ignore her clit to plunge two fingers inside her. Her back bows off the bed.

"Is this what you want?" I ask as I pump my fingers into her.

"More."

I pinch her nipple with one hand while I increase the tempo of my thrusts into her pussy with the other. The combination is too much for her and she comes all over my hand.

"Brody!" she shouts.

"There you go. Shout my name when you come," I encourage.

"Brody, Brody, Brody," she chants as I draw out her orgasm with my fingers.

"Wow," she slurs once her climax finishes.

I reach up with my free hand to remove her blindfold before withdrawing my fingers from her pussy and licking them. Her eyes flare as she watches me.

I open the handcuffs and check the skin on her wrists. "Wait here."

"Wait here for what?"

I don't answer her as I stroll to the bathroom to start a bath for her. I return to the bedroom and lift her from the bed.

"What are we doing now?"

"You're having a bath to soothe your skin from the wax."

"Will you join me?" she asks as I place her in the water.

"You couldn't stop me if you tried," I say as I climb in behind her.

I wrap my arms around her and she lays her head against my shoulder. My cock aches. It doesn't help when she wiggles her ass against me.

"Aren't we going to handle that little problem you have?"

I bite her shoulder. "Not a little problem. And we will handle it. But first I'm going to take care of you."

My cock can wait. The most important thing is to make sure Soleil is okay after the wax play. I'm not going to force the woman I love to do things in the bedroom she doesn't want to do. I'll make certain she's in a good frame of mind. Then, I'm going to make love to the woman I love.

Chapter 30

I SIGH AS THE arm wrapped around me tightens and Brody snuggles closer into me. There's nowhere else in the world I'd rather be. I don't have the urge to jump out of bed and work on my pottery. I want to stay here. Forever.

Whoa, Soleil. What are you thinking? Do you love Brody?

Do I love the way he makes me feel good? Do I love the way he takes care of me? Cooking for me? Cleaning the house for me?

Well, crap. This is unexpected. Completely and totally unexpected.

I didn't expect to fall in love with the juvenile prankster who's way too young for me. *Knock it off, Soleil.* Brody is way more than a prankster. And he's certainly not juvenile. Especially not when he shows you how much pleasure he can bring you in the bedroom. And he's not too young for me. He's not my dad.

"What are you thinking about over there?" he asks before kissing my ear.

"Nothing," I mutter before I can blurt out how much I love him.

He chuckles. "Which is why there's smoke coming out of your ears."

I roll until I'm facing him. "Smoke isn't coming out of my ears."

He tweaks my nose. "Sure, it isn't."

"You're annoying in the morning."

"I think you mean adorable."

I roll my eyes. "Awful full of yourself, aren't you?"

He smirks. "No, but I—"

I slap my hand over his mouth before he starts with the sex talk. It's super sexy at night when he has me all tied up and blindfolded, but in the morning light? I'm going to need some time before I get used to Brody the prankster also being Brody the sexy talker.

"It's too early in the morning for whatever annoying thing you were going to say. It's only…," I check the clock and let out a yelp. "Oh no. It's already eight. I should be at work. The kiln should already be ready to go. I'm late."

I roll to get out of bed but Brody shackles my wrist to stop me. "What are you doing?"

"You can't leave this bed until you kiss me good morning."

I narrow my eyes on him. "Is this a rule?" He nods. "When did this become a rule?"

"This very second."

"You are literally the most annoying person in the world in the morning." I peck his mouth and turn to leave but he stops me again.

"That is not a morning kiss."

"What are you? The morning kiss police? Are you going to issue me a citation for not kissing you properly?"

"No, but I will smack your ass for sassing me."

My body tingles in anticipation, but Soleil Hawk does not give in. Ever. "You can try," I sass before yanking my hand away and jumping out of bed.

I don't make it to the door before Brody's on me. He wraps his arms around me before spinning me around and pushing me up against the wall.

"How's this for trying?" he grumbles before his mouth crashes against mine.

This isn't some simple peck on the mouth. Brody pushes his tongue into my mouth before commencing to devour me. I should be ashamed about my morning breath but I can't find the mental capacity to care. Not when I can feel his hard length pressing against my stomach causing excitement to build inside of me.

I'm ready to say forget work when he pulls away. "Now, that's how you say good morning to your boyfriend." I nod since I'm currently incapable of speech. "I'll make breakfast while you get ready for the day."

He strolls away and I watch as he reaches down to grab a pair of boxers from the floor. I can't look away from those strong muscles on display.

He glances over his shoulder and winks. "Aren't you running late?"

Late? Shit. I am. "This is all your fault." I hurry to the bathroom. I can hear his laughter through the closed door.

I quickly empty my protesting bladder before brushing my teeth and throwing my hair up into a bun. There. Ready for a day of throwing pots.

I catch sight of my reflection in the mirror and pause when I notice the crow's feet around my eyes. I frown causing wrinkles around my mouth to appear. Maybe Brody isn't too young for me. Maybe I'm too old for him.

Maybe I'm merely a fling to him. Why the hell did I go and fall in love with the man? This is going to be a disaster.

I inhale a deep breath. Now is not the time to have a breakdown about my age and having a younger boyfriend. I need to get to work. I have pottery orders to fill. I straighten my back and march out of the bathroom.

Brody smiles at me when I enter the kitchen. He certainly doesn't have any wrinkles around his eyes or mouth.

Before I know what's happening, Brody's standing in front of me, and my back is to the counter.

"What's wrong?"

"Why do you think anything's wrong?"

"Because when I left the bedroom, you had the look of a well-satisfied woman. Now, you appear terrified."

I scowl. "I'm not terrified."

He cocks an eyebrow. "No?"

"I'm worried about how far behind I am on my pottery orders." It's true. I am. Even if it's not what I was thinking about when I entered the kitchen.

He cradles my face. "How can I help? I can phone your customers and explain the delay. I'm sure they'll understand."

"You don't need to ring my customers for me."

"I don't know how else I can help."

"You don't need to help. I'll figure it out."

He studies my face for a few moments before nodding. "Okay, pixie. But promise me you'll let me know if there's anything I can do."

I open my mouth to say *I love you* but manage to choke down the words before they can escape. Brody will run as far and as fast as he can if I admit to my feelings. It's way too early in our relationship for love. We barely know each other.

"I'll let you know," I push the words out.

"Good." He kisses my nose. "I made French toast with extra cinnamon for breakfast."

"Extra cinnamon? You really know the way to a girl's heart."

Oh no. I need to backtrack and erase those words. But before I can think of a way to soften the blow, Brody speaks.

"That's the idea, pixie girl. That's the idea."

The idea? Does he mean he wants me to fall in love with him?

I shake my head. Since when am I *that* girl? The one who rehashes every single word a man says to her. *Enough, Soleil.*

"Sit down and I'll bring you a coffee while I finish the French toast."

"Bossy Brody has arrived at the party."

His eyes heat. "Bossy Brody is always at the party."

"It wasn't a compliment."

He swats my ass. "Yes, it was."

"Whatever," I mutter as I sit down.

He sets a cup of coffee in front of me. "This should help with your sassiness."

I drink half of the cup in one go. "I'm not sassy."

He chuckles. "And I'm not bossy."

I have no response since he is super bossy in bed. And I enjoy the hell out of it. Although, you'll never hear me admit it outside of the bedroom. "I thought you were making me breakfast."

"I'm supposed to be the bossy one."

"Boss your way across the kitchen to the stove and get me my French toast, then."

"I think you're confused about what bossy means," he mutters as he grabs a plate from the cupboard. He places two pieces of French toast on the plate before setting it in front of me.

I sniff. "Smells yummy."

He nudges the plate closer. "Eat. You're running late, remember?"

How did I forget I'm running late? Maybe Brody shouldn't be Bossy Brody but Make Me Forget Everything But Him Brody. I have to admit Brody making me forget about all my troubles at night is one of the reasons I love him.

My heart batters against my ribcage. I need some time to get used to the idea of loving Brody Bragg, the youngest Bragg who thinks pranking is an expression of love.

Chapter 31

BRODY

"Are you sure Soleil will love this?" I ask Moon on the phone as I stare at the kitchen counter, which is currently covered in various ingredients for dinner as well as pots and pans and a mini torch. The mini torch concerns me.

"Why don't I prepare the dinner for you?" Moon asks.

"What? No! I want to do this for Soleil to show her how special she is to me. Asking you to prepare a meal doesn't say special."

"This is awesome! Soleil finally found her man."

"What? No! I'm not her man," I deny, although I am definitely her man. But I can't let Soleil's friends catch on to how much I love her before I tell her.

"You're her boyfriend, aren't you?"

"I'm not a boy."

"You have all the boy parts, don't you?"

I growl. "I have the man parts."

"I can't wait to tell Ashlyn."

"You can't tattle to Ashlyn about tonight. I want this meal to be a surprise for Soleil."

I want tonight to be special because tonight's the night. I'm going to tell Soleil I love her. My heart thumps in my chest and my hands clam up. I wipe them on my jeans. No clammy hands while cooking.

"I'm not going to tell Soleil."

"Ashlyn has the biggest mouth in Winter Falls. If you tell her about tonight, Soleil will find out."

Don't get me wrong. Ashlyn is fun. But she has no idea what the word discretion means. Not the first clue.

"I can't believe you," Moon grumbles.

Crap. I forgot Moon and Ashlyn are attached at the hip.

"I'm sorry. I didn't mean to bad mouth your best friend."

"You can bad mouth Ashlyn all you want. I can't believe you think she has the biggest mouth in Winter Falls. What about me?"

"You're my favorite sister-in-law," I claim, although she has yet to marry Riley. They will, though. My twin learned his lesson. He's not letting Moon go again.

"Can I tell Harmony and Eden what you said?"

I groan. "You're a shit stirrer."

"Thank you."

"I have to go. I need to get started on dinner."

I glance at the clock. An hour to make a rack of lamb, homemade mashed potatoes, and salad for dinner? I can do this. But the crème brulee? I'm still not sure about using a mini torch.

When the doorbell rings forty-five minutes later, the mashed potatoes are made and the rack of lamb is resting on the kitchen counter. I shove the croutons in the oven to toast them before answering the door.

"I can't believe Moon," I grumble when I open the door to the gossip gal gang standing on the porch.

"What about Moon?" Sage asks as she pushes her way inside with Feather, Petal, Cayenne, and Clove following her.

"Why don't you come in?"

"Keep up the sarcasm and we won't help you finish your special dinner for Soleil," Cayenne says as she marches to the kitchen.

I hurry after her. "I don't need your help."

"Yummy," Clove mumbles around a spoon.

I snatch the spoon from her hand. "What are you doing? You can't stick your spoon into a bowl of mashed potatoes."

She shrugs. "How else can I taste whether they're any good?"

"You don't need to taste whether they're good."

"Disagree," she says as she sticks a different spoon into the juice around the lamb.

"Where did you get this spoon?" I ask as I bat her away from the rack of lamb.

"I always come prepared with my own utensils."

Feather nods in agreement. "It's good practice to avoid using the plastic junk you get at some restaurants."

"I'm going to kill Moon," I grumble.

"What have you got against Moon?" Sage asks.

"She's a tattletale who told you I'm making a special dinner for Soleil tonight."

Sage holds her palm out to Petal. "You owe me twenty dollars."

Petal snorts. "I didn't bet against you. Everyone knows Brody is making a special dinner for Soleil tonight."

I bury my face in my hands with a groan. "This is supposed to be a surprise."

Feather pats my back. "Don't worry. It is."

I lift my head. "Really? Moon didn't tell the entire town by now?"

Sage scowls. "Why do you keep saying Moon told everyone? We have our own sources."

I cross my arms over my chest. "Really? Who's your source if it isn't Moon?"

"You ordered a rack of lamb from Shine at *Nature Coop*."

I will never buy my groceries in Winter Falls again. No one in this town can keep a secret.

"And no one buys a rack of lamb for a Tuesday night unless it's a special occasion," Cayenne continues.

"I hope the special occasion is them using the candles I made them," Petal says.

"You made us candles?" I deflect.

She wags her finger at me. "Don't lie to me. I know you got the basket I left you. I watched you with my binoculars myself."

Sage gasps. "You're the one who's been hogging the binoculars!"

Petal shrugs. "I need them the most."

"We agreed the binoculars would be shared equally amongst the five of us."

"We agreed?" Petal snorts. "You mean you laid down the law and no one was allowed to say otherwise."

"I'll buy each of you a pair of binoculars if you agree to leave this house now," I interrupt to offer.

Cayenne pats my cheek. "Isn't he cute?"

"And he can cook, too," Clove adds as she licks her spoon.

"What did you stick your spoon in now?"

She motions toward the small bowl next to the salad I still haven't finished preparing. "The salad dressing. Although I prefer a balsamic vinaigrette, the red wine goes well with the lamb."

"I love red wine vinaigrette." Cayenne pushes her way past Clove. "I want to try."

"No one's trying anything!" I shout. "Soleil is going to be here any minute and I still need to finish prepping the meal and set the table."

I try to herd them toward the front door but they refuse to move. Short of picking them up and throwing them out the door, I don't know what to do.

"Which is why we're here," Sage says.

"To help you get everything prepared," Petal adds.

I inhale a deep breath before I tell them I would already be prepared if it weren't for their intrusion.

Clove sniffs. "What am I smelling?"

"Is something burning?" Cayenne asks.

"Nothing's burning. Everything's out of the oven." I turn to check if the oven is turned off and notice smoke emitting from it. "Shit. The croutons!"

I yank the oven door open and smoke pours out of it. I grab an oven mitt, remove the tray of croutons, and set it on the stove before switching off the oven and shutting the door. And here I was worried about the mini torch.

"I'll phone River. I have the sexy volunteer fireman on speed dial." Petal digs her phone out of her purse.

"There's no need to phone the fire department for a few burnt croutons," I argue.

The smoke alarm goes off to prove me wrong. I grab a towel and wave it in front of the alarm.

"I'll alert River just in case," Petal says as she dials her phone.

"We should evacuate the building," Sage shouts over the alarm.

"There's no need to evacuate. There's smoke but no fire." I glance at the croutons on the stove. Okay, fine. More than a bit of smoke. But there's no fire. I'm firm on the lack of fire.

"What's going on?" River shouts as he runs into the house in full fireman gear minus the helmet.

"Everything is under control," I yell over the sound of the smoke alarm.

"I'll show you what the problem is, River." Petal bats her eyelashes at him.

River fists his hands at his hips. "Petal, you promised to stop phoning in false alarms."

"It's not a false alarm. The smoke alarm is going off and the oven's on fire."

"The oven is not on fire."

"The oven's on fire?" Soleil screeches as she rushes inside. "What happened?"

The smoke alarm cuts off.

"Nothing. Everything's fine," I claim despite the smoke lingering in the room.

"Make sure you ventilate the house well tonight and throw away whatever that is." River indicates the croutons on the oven. I can't blame him for not recognizing the food. It's a charred mess.

"Come on ladies, I'll escort you out."

The gossip gals rush to him. They wave as they leave.

"Have fun!"

"Don't do anything I wouldn't do!"

"Don't forget about our binoculars!"

The door shuts behind them and I grin at Soleil. "There's a reasonable explanation."

Chapter 32

"A REASONABLE EXPLANATION?" I grit my teeth to stop myself from exploding.

"The gossip gals stopped by and—"

"You're blaming this on the gossip gals?"

"No. I mean it was kind of their fault."

"Real mature. You cause a fire and blame it on five sweet elderly women."

"Hey now. No one can seriously refer to the gossip gals as sweet."

"And now you're throwing shade on the gossip gals!"

"If you'd let me explain."

"Let you explain," I sneer. "I don't need an explanation. You were obviously up to your old tricks."

"My old tricks?"

I poke him. "Don't act innocent. You know what your old tricks are. Pulling pranks and causing fires. I should have known better. I must have been crazy to get involved with you."

"I wasn't pulling a prank."

"You weren't? Really? Need I remind you how I arrived home to discover the fire department all over my house!"

"It wasn't the fire department. It was River."

"River is *the* fire department."

"Petal phoned him because she thinks he's sexy. There was no need for the fire department."

"Now you're blaming Petal for your mistakes?"

He runs a hand through his hair and yanks. I ignore how frustrated he is. How dare he be frustrated? I'm the one who came home after a long day of work to my house on fire.

"I'm not blaming anyone. I'm trying to explain what happened."

"I don't need an explanation. I can clearly see exactly what happened." I motion toward whatever the hell is burned on top of my stove.

"They're croutons for on top of the salad. I was preparing a—"

I hold up my hand to stop him. "I don't want to hear it."

"You're overreacting."

"I'm overreacting?" I pound my fist to my chest. "I'm overreacting?"

Brody reaches for me but I bat his hands away.

"How dare you say I'm overreacting? I'm the one who came home to discover my pottery shed burned down and now I come home to this."

"Fuck," he mutters. "I didn't think—"

"Exactly my point. You never think. You never think of anyone except yourself. You need to grow the hell up."

"I am a grown man," he grumbles.

"Age has nothing to do with maturity level." My nostrils flare. "I can't believe you conned me into believing there was more to you than your childish pranks. You're just like my dad. And I'm an idiot."

"You're not an idiot," he growls, "and I'm not your dad. There is more to me than childish pranks, which this was not by the way."

"I don't believe you," I say as I retreat several steps. I can't do what needs to be done while I'm sniffing his sandalwood scent. "I think you should leave."

"Leave? You want me to leave?" Confusion clouds his vision.

I stare at a point over his shoulder. I refuse to be pulled in by those baby blue eyes staring at me with hurt in them. "At the risk of repeating myself, yes, I want you to leave."

He blows out a breath. "Okay. I can go for a walk while you have a shower."

I don't want him to leave for a few hours. I want him to leave forever. Before he can pull me further into his trap. I never should have fallen in love with him. No, I didn't fall in love with him. I fell in love with a version of him. A version of him that doesn't exist as it turns out.

Is this what happened to my mom? Did she get fooled by Dad?

"No." My jaw is clenched so hard I'm surprised he can understand me.

"You need more time? I can hang out with Elder and Miller at *Naked Falls Brewing* for a few hours."

"I'm not talking about a few hours."

His nose scrunches up. "You want me to find somewhere else to sleep for the night? Okay. Let me pack an overnight bag." His shoulders hunch.

I refuse to let his defeated appearance sway me. He's not the injured party here. I am. What happens the next time he plays with fire? I've already lost a bed and a pottery shed. I can't lose this house. This is the house my mom raised me in. She left it to me. I need to protect it.

"You don't need an overnight bag!"

He holds up his hands and backs away. "Okay. Okay. I can borrow a toothbrush from Riley."

Why is he not getting what I'm saying? Is he messing with me? Probably. It's what he does after all. "Are you deliberately being obtuse?"

He scratches his ear. "No?"

I push up on my toes and get into his face. "I want you to leave. Forever."

"Forever?" The color drains from his face. "You're breaking up with me?"

"What was your first clue?"

"You can't break up with me."

"Not only can I break up with you. I *am* breaking up with you."

He captures my wrists in his hands. "But I love you."

I flinch. I dreamed of him saying those words to me. But not this way. Not in an attempt to manipulate me into getting what he wants.

"You love me? How dare you claim to love me now! Stop trying to manipulate me."

"I'm not trying to manipulate you. I love you. You have my heart, pixie girl."

"I am not your pixie girl." I yank away from his hold. "You don't love me. You love living in my house rent-free. You love having no responsibilities."

"I have responsibilities. I have a job."

I snort. "A job? You play computer games for a living."

Hurt flashes in his eyes but I will not be affected by his hurt. I need to protect myself. I need to be number one in my life for a change.

"And I offered to pay rent."

"I can't accept rent from you when you're not earning much money."

He scowls. "Why do you assume I don't earn much money?"

I roll my eyes. "Because..." I trail off when I realize we're arguing about his financial situation. His financial situation is not the topic I want to discuss.

"Your bank account is not the issue."

"It sounds as if you have a problem with my finances."

"Don't distract me." I point to the door. "You need to leave."

"This isn't fair. I make one mistake and you kick me out? You didn't even let me explain what happened."

"Did you forget about the first bed you ruined?"

"I admit I messed up with the bed. I should have never been messing around with fireworks in the house. But I wasn't messing around with fireworks now. I learned my lesson."

I point to the kitchen. "I beg to differ."

"Let me explain."

I hold up my palm. There's no reason to explain. It's plain to see what happened here. And I can't chance it happening again. I need to stand firm. I can't risk coming home to firemen in my house again. I just can't. This house is all I have left of my mom.

"Here." He grasps my hand and tugs me toward the kitchen. "Let me show you at least."

I wrest my hand from his grip. "No. You need to leave."

"Can we please sit down and discuss this like adults?"

"Like adults?" I throw my hands in the air. "That's the whole problem. You're not an adult. You're a child."

"I am not a child," he growls.

"Fine." I give in since I don't want to have this discussion yet again. "You're not a child. But you're too young for me. I thought I could handle the age difference. I can't. I was wrong."

I twirl around and march toward our bedroom. No, not our bedroom. *My* bedroom.

"I'll be at the community center all day tomorrow. You can come get your stuff then."

"Are you serious? I thought I was the child. But you're the one stomping away like a child because I made one mistake."

I whirl around. "How dare you say I'm a child?"

"If you'll only let me explain," he pleads.

I don't respond. I'm done talking. All talking does is lead me to question my decision. I can't question my decision. Brody is not the man I thought he was.

He pretended to be the man I wanted. Pretended to be an adult. But it was only a façade. The real Brody is immature. A prankster who will never grow up. He's not for me. I need him gone before I repeat the mistake my mom made.

I slam the bedroom door and collapse against it. I wait until I hear the front door shut before sliding to the floor.

Damn him. I never should have let him past my defenses.

Chapter 33

"Soleil!"

I groan when Harmony shouts my name. It hasn't even been an hour since I kicked Brody out and the news has already spread all over town. Sometimes living in a small town sucks.

"I'll check the bedroom," Ashlyn says.

Ugh. The last thing I want is for my friends to invade my house for some sort of cheer me up ritual. I pull the cover up over my face. Maybe if I can't see Ashlyn, she won't be able to see me?

"Aha!" she shouts as she yanks the covers off me. "Found her!"

I glare at her. "Do you always have to shout?"

"Yes, I do." She grins. "Thank you for noticing."

I throw my pillow at her. "It wasn't a compliment."

Harmony peeks inside the room. "Are we meeting in here?" She doesn't wait for an answer before yelling behind her. "We're meeting in Soleil's bedroom."

Harmony climbs onto the bed and settles next to me while Eden, Moon, and Ashlyn sit at my feet. At least I don't have to get out of bed for this cheer me up session.

"What happened?" Ashlyn asks.

"I thought we were going to ease into it before we started interrogating her," Eden says.

"Interrogating? Am I suspect? What's my crime?" I try to make light of the situation since I have no desire to discuss my break-up with Brody.

"Breaking Brody's heart," Moon says.

I scowl. "I didn't break Brody's heart."

She snorts. "Sure, you didn't. And he didn't show up at our house all teary-eyed asking for sanctuary."

"Sanctuary? He's not a political refugee."

"Maybe he's seeking refuge from the wrath of Soleil," Ashlyn suggests.

I roll my eyes. "The wrath of Soleil? What am I? Some kind of angry beast?"

She shrugs. "Rumor has it you were pretty pissed when you arrived home tonight."

I don't bother asking how she knows I was pissed when I got home. This is Winter Falls after all. "Wouldn't you be pissed if the fire department was in your house when you got home after a long day of work?"

"I don't know. River is pretty hot in his fireman outfit."

"I'm telling Rowan what you said."

She grins. "Good. It's been a while since my husband gave me a good punishment."

I bury my face in my hands. "Someone stop her before she starts describing her sex life. I can't handle it."

"I heard otherwise," Eden says.

I lift my head. "Don't be coy. Say what you mean."

She grins. "I heard someone enjoyed Petal's candles."

I growl. "I'm going to kill Brody for telling people about our sex life. After him, I'll start on his brothers."

"Whoa!" Harmony raises her hands. "Leave Elder out of this. He didn't do anything wrong."

"Elder didn't tell anyone anything," Eden says. "And before you start complaining about Miller or Riley, they didn't tell anyone anything about your sex life either."

"Then, how do you know?"

She smiles. "Because you just confirmed you used the candles Petal left in a basket on your porch when you jumped down my throat."

"You tricked me!"

Ashlyn clutches her chest. "I'm so proud of you, Eden."

Eden bows. "Thank you. You have to be tricky when you're engaged to a Bragg brother."

"Or married to one," Harmony adds.

"I'm not engaged or married to a Bragg brother, so I'll leave the tricks to you," I say.

"And why aren't you engaged, or married, or living with a Bragg brother?" Moon asks. "Brody is pretty sexy considering he's a carbon copy of Riley."

Ashlyn raises her hand. "I have a question."

Moon nods to her. "Go ahead."

"If Brody and Riley are identical twins, are they identical everywhere? Including their equipment and its size?" I choke on my own spit. "What?" She shrugs. "I'm curious. My mom says there's nothing wrong with curiosity."

"Your mom also spends the majority of her life trying to convince people to use birth control," I point out.

"Birth control is important."

"I have to admit," Eden begins. "Now, I'm curious, too."

Harmony shakes her head. "No way. I'm not discussing how big Elder is down there."

"Down there." Ashlyn snickers. "It's a cock, Harmony. You have a child. I'm pretty sure you know what one is."

Harmony glares at her. "I don't have a child. I'm the guardian of my cousin's daughter."

"I stand by my point. You know what a cock is."

Harmony rolls her eyes. "Of course, I do. But I'm not going to compare Elder and Miller's sizes. Besides, they're fraternal twins. They're not identical."

"But Riley and Brody are." Ashlyn focuses on me. "So, tell me. Are they identical in size?"

"How would I know? I've never seen Riley naked."

"What about you Moon?"

Moon snorts. "I've never seen Brody naked. And, just to make this crystal clear, I never want to see Brody naked."

I glare at her. "What's wrong with seeing Brody naked?"

Eden claps. "Finally. We're back to the matter at hand."

Shit. I should have kept my big mouth shut.

"What's the matter at hand?"

"I'm not going to dignify your question with an answer. Now, tell us what happened."

"Yeah." Ashlyn nods. "Why did you kick Brody to the curb?"

"And is it true the gossip gals witnessed the entire thing?" Moon asks.

I hold up my hands as if to ward off their questions. "Hey! This is supposed to be a cheer me up session. Not a Soleil is an idiot session."

Eden shrugs. "Why can't it be both?"

"You're going to give us the dirt eventually. Why not rip off the bandage right away?" Harmony asks.

I contemplate my group of girlfriends sitting on my bed eagerly awaiting my response. I can evade their questions for a while, but Harmony's correct, I'll give in eventually. If only to get Moon and Ashlyn off my back.

"Fine," I huff. "What do you want to know?"

Eden doesn't hesitate. "Why did you break up with the man you love?"

"I don't love Brody."

Ashlyn sighs. "This is going to be a long night. Did someone bring booze?"

"It's true. I don't love Brody," I continue to lie.

"And I don't love to cook," Moon says.

"And I don't love plants," Eden says.

"And I don't love animals," Harmony says.

"And I'm not awesome," Ashlyn says. Moon smacks her. "What? Everyone's stating falsehoods to show Soleil what an idiot she is. I'm awesome. Therefore, saying I'm not awesome is a falsehood."

Moon groans. "I just can't with you."

"Twenty dollars says Soleil lies about loving Brody for the next thirty minutes," Ashlyn says.

"Fine! I love Brody. Are you happy now?"

She smirks. "Very happy. I tricked you."

Moon holds out her hand. "You owe me twenty dollars."

"And me," Eden adds.

Harmony waves her hand. "Don't forget me."

"Another twenty bucks says Soleil broke up with Brody because she got scared," Ashlyn proposes.

"It's like taking candy from a baby." Moon chuckles. "Of course, she broke up with Brody because she got scared."

"Hey! I'm not scared."

Harmony bumps my shoulder. "It's natural to be scared."

Eden nods. "Falling in love is scary."

Ashlyn raises her hand. "I didn't find it scary."

Moon slams a hand over Ashlyn's mouth. "Ignore her. She's not normal."

I'm getting annoyed with all of this. "I'm not scared. Brody tried to burn my house down. The house my mother left me. It's the only thing I have left of her. I'm not letting some asshole burn it down because he's an immature idiot who thinks pulling pranks is funny. He reminds me of my dad."

"Your dad?" Eden barks out a laugh. "I was still a teenager when he fled town after your mom died but even I can remember what a lazy asshole he was."

"I remember him, too," Moon says. "Brody is not similar to him in any manner whatsoever."

Ashlyn nods. "Agreed."

"Good. We've established Brody is not your dad. Moving on."

I glare at Harmony. "There's nowhere to move on to. It's over and done with. Brody and I are no longer."

Eden clears her throat. "How about how she's lying to herself about what happened because she's scared of falling in love with Brody?"

I point at her. "You're one to talk. You were terrified of being in a relationship with Miller."

"Exactly. I'm speaking from experience. It's scary falling in love but making yourself vulnerable to another person is also the greatest reward you can imagine."

It doesn't matter how reasonable she sounds. She's wrong. Our situations are completely different. Miller isn't a prankster who tried to burn down her house.

"Did you forget how Brody tried to burn down my house?"

Harmony pats my hand. "He didn't try to burn down your house. He was making you a special dinner."

"How do you know?"

She points at Moon. "Because she was his sous chef."

Moon sniffs. "I'm no one's sous chef, but I was his special advisor."

I open my mouth to ask about the special meal but snap it closed again when I realize it doesn't matter.

"Regardless, Brody is not the man for me."

Ashlyn sighs. "If she's continuing down the stubborn path, can we at least eat?"

Moon stands from the bed. "I made a charcuterie board."

I follow her. Food sounds great since I missed dinner. I plop down on the sofa while she retrieves the food from the kitchen table.

"What did you make?" I ask as she sets a large cutting board on the coffee table.

"A little bit of everything. I'll fix you a plate."

She places cheeses and meats on the plate before handing it to me. I pick up a deviled egg but when the scent invades my nose nausea hits me. I jump to my feet and run to the bathroom where I promptly expel everything in my stomach.

Chapter 34

When I finally finish heaving into the toilet, I collapse next to it and lay my head on the seat.

"I swear the eggs aren't rotten," Moon says.

I glance behind me and notice everyone followed me into the bathroom. I should have run for the half bath in the hallway. All of my friends couldn't fit in there.

"Nope. They're actually really good," Ashlyn says around a mouthful of food.

I glare at her. "What? They are. I can't help it you're preggers."

Preggers? Joy overcomes me at the idea. A child of my own. My dream come true. Reality knocks on the door to remind me I can't be pregnant.

"I'm not pregnant. I can't be."

"Can't be?" Eden raises her eyebrows. "I thought you and Brody have been having sex."

Ashlyn rocks her hips. "Knocking boots. Baking the potato. Buttering the biscuit. Getting your kettle mended."

Moon places a hand over Ashlyn's mouth. "Now is not the time to impress us with how many euphemisms for having sex you know."

Ashlyn pushes Moon's hand away. "But you were impressed. My work here is done." She bows.

"We have been having sex, but we use protection."

"Protection isn't fool proof. Ask my sister, Ellery. She was on the pill *and* they used a condom but she still got pregnant. Fine by me. Willow is absolutely adorable."

Condom? Shit. Brody forgot a condom the first time we had sex.

"Fuck."

"Uh oh. Mama's using the f bomb," Moon mutters.

Eden kneels in front of me and places a cold washcloth on my forehead. "What is it? What are you thinking?"

"I'm thinking Brody's an irresponsible man–child who forgot to use a condom the first time we had sex."

Harmony claps. "Yeah! Robin will have a cousin to play with."

Ashlyn scowls. "Robin already has a cousin to play with. My daughter Patience."

"A Bragg cousin I mean."

Ashlyn narrows her eyes on Harmony. "Are you prejudiced against my family?"

Eden sighs. "How do you do it? Keep all of us in line all the time?" she asks me.

I shrug. It comes naturally to me since taking care of people is what I do.

Moon clears her throat. "I hate to be the voice of reason here, but maybe we should find out if Soleil is pregnant for sure before we begin plotting ways to make Brody's life hell."

"I wasn't plotting ways to make Brody's life hell." I wasn't. But now I am.

Eden stands. "I got this. I'll buy a pregnancy test and be right back."

I clutch her hand before she can leave. "You can't buy a pregnancy test in Winter Falls. Everyone will know."

"It's okay. Everyone knows Miller and I are trying."

She's not getting what I'm saying. "But everyone will think you're pregnant."

She flinches. "Don't worry. Miller knows I'm not pregnant."

I squeeze her hand. "I'm sorry. Do you want to leave? Is this bringing up too much shit for you?"

She smiles at me. "Always mothering us even when you're lying on the floor of your bathroom puking your guts out."

"I think I'm done puking."

"Ha!" Ashlyn chuckles. "If you are pregnant, you won't be done puking until the baby comes out. Have fun."

Eden pats my hand. "I'll be right back."

"Let's calculate the odds of Soleil being pregnant," Ashlyn suggests once Eden is gone.

"Calculate the odds? Did you forget you suck at math?" Moon asks.

"I don't suck at math."

"Why did you cheat on all your math tests if you don't suck at math?"

Ashlyn wiggles her eyebrows. "Maybe I was aiming for Rowan to tutor me."

Moon snorts. "Try again. Rowan was in college when we were in high school."

Harmony joins me on the floor. "You must be feeling like complete shit if you're not shutting down the Ashlyn and Moon show."

"It's keeping me distracted," I admit.

"Do you think it's true Ashlyn tried to kiss Rowan when she was in sixth grade and he was a senior in high school?" she asks.

"I think it's a miracle Rowan's ex-wife is still alive."

Ashlyn smirks. "Who says the bitch is still alive?"

"Um, me?" Moon raises her hand. "Since you never asked me to help you bury the body."

"Maybe I buried the body on my own."

"Ha! You get dirt under your fingernails?"

"I used to get dirt under my fingernails all the time when we'd sneak off after my older sister and her boyfriend to find out what they did when they were alone."

Moon waves a hand in front of her face. "Aspen and Lyric together were hot. I'm glad they figured out their shit and got married."

Harmony leans close to whisper to me, "My brain hurts from trying to follow their conversation."

Before I can agree, Eden rushes into the room. "I did it! No one saw me come here."

"And if they did, they'll think the test is for you. Sneaky. I knew there was a reason I liked you," Ashlyn says.

"Shine only had three kinds of pregnancy tests at *Nature Coop*," Eden says as she lays them on the vanity.

"I'm surprised she has any at all," I say.

Moon snorts. "Are you serious? The gossip gals insisted she stock them because they're, quote 'ready for grandchildren' end quote."

"Ready for grandchildren?" Ashlyn's nose scrunches. "They already have grandchildren. I have a kid and two of my sisters have kids."

Moon shrugs. "She probably meant more grandchildren."

"I don't—"

"Enough!" I shout. "I appreciate you putting on the Moon and Ashlyn show to distract me while we waited for Eden to return, but enough is enough."

"You're going to be a great mom," Eden says and everyone nods in agreement.

My entire body vibrates in excitement at the idea of having a child. But I force myself to hold onto reality. There's no child yet.

"Let's not put the cart before the horse." I stand. "Now everyone out. I need to pee on a stick."

Harmony herds everyone out the door.

"I don't understand why we need to leave. I've seen a woman pee before. She has all the same parts as we do," Ashlyn whines.

I wait until the door closes. I quickly lock it – I wouldn't put it past Ashlyn to barge inside – before opening the pregnancy tests and getting to work.

"You doing okay in there?" Harmony calls through the door.

"I have a timer on my phone you can use," Ashlyn says.

"I'm fine," I lie. My hands are clammy, I feel nauseous again, and my heart is about to beat its way out of my chest.

"It's been four minutes. If you wait too long to check your results, they may be inaccurate," Ashlyn hollers.

"Now, she understands science," I mutter as I force myself to stand and look at the pregnancy tests.

I did all three. Of course, I did. I need an accurate result. One of them could be faulty. Or give a false positive. Shit. Can all three give a false positive at the same time?

Pregnant. I'm pregnant? Elation wars with worry and fear. Now is not the best time for me to be pregnant. My pottery business is in turmoil since my shed burned down and I just broke up with my boyfriend. No, not boyfriend. The father of my child.

My stomach rolls and I dive for the toilet before the heaving can begin. The bathroom door flies open behind me.

I motion for them to leave. "Go away."

Eden places a cold washcloth on my neck while Harmony pulls back my hair. "We're not going anywhere," she says.

"Uh oh. Someone's got a bun in the oven," Ashlyn announces.

I finish dry heaving into the toilet. When I manage to compose myself, I narrow my eyes on her.

"What?" She points to the vanity. "You left the tests out."

I groan. "What am I going to do?"

"Easy. Be a great mom," Moon says.

"Yeah. You've been mothering us for as long as I can remember," Ashlyn agrees.

Harmony nods. "It's good you have experience. No experience totally sucks."

"I meant about Brody. He's too young to be a father."

"Hold up. Brody's older than me," Ashlyn points out.

"And me," Moon agrees.

Harmony crosses her arms over her chest. "And me."

Eden squeezes my hands. "You love Brody. This is a good thing."

"Did you forget I broke up with Brody because he tried to burn my house down?"

Moon frowns at me. "He wasn't trying to burn your house down. He even refused to use the mini torch for the crème brulee."

Ashlyn sits on the ground next to me. "It's okay to be scared. Becoming a mom is scary."

"And falling in love is scary," Harmony adds.

I don't know what I'm going to do, but one thing is certain. I want my pregnancy to be a secret for the time being. "You can't tell your partners about the baby."

"I'm not a snitch," Ashlyn claims. She's the biggest snitch of all. Except she calls it gossiping, which somehow makes it okay in her opinion. It's not.

"We won't tell any of the Bragg brothers," Moon promises.

"Or Peace."

She rolls her eyes. "Or Peace."

"Or Daisy Bragg."

"Why don't we just agree to keep this a secret until you're ready to tell Brody?" Harmony suggests.

I study my friends. "I'm not sure anyone in Winter Falls can keep a secret."

"Hey! I never told anyone about the time Moon got drunk and thought she could fly," Ashlyn claims.

I snort. "You didn't need to tell anyone since Moon broke her arm and had to go to the emergency room."

"And you pushed me," Moon says.

Ashlyn shrugs. "I helped you figure out if you can fly. Spoiler alert – you can't."

My stomach rumbles and I groan. "Not again."

Moon offers me her hand. "Come on. I'll get you some dry crackers and ginger ale."

Ashlyn rubs her hands together. "Awesome. More food for me."

I shake my head. Some things never change. I glance around at my friends. I hope things never change between us. Despite our various ages and interests, the five of us have maintained our friendship throughout the years. Fingers crossed nothing changes since they now have partners and I apparently am going to have a family.

I force the baby out of my mind. I have plenty of time to contemplate what to do when I'm alone. For now, I'll let my friends distract me from reality. Tomorrow reality is up to bat.

Chapter 35

BRODY

"How did you find me?" I ask when the front door opens and my brothers invade Harmony's house where I'm currently squatting.

Elder chuckles. "Are you kidding? You're sitting in my wife's house. Of course, we found you."

"Was it the gossip gals or you?" I ask Peace.

He shrugs. "You walked through the goat farm on the way here. Phoenix phoned it in to the station."

Riley plops down next to me. "I thought you were allergic to dogs."

"You knew I wasn't."

Sue me. I lied. How else was I going to convince Soleil to let me live with her? The woman fascinated me from the moment I met her but she wouldn't give me the time of day. So, I came up with a plan to make her pay attention to me.

I lift my bottle, but before it can reach my lips, Peace snatches it from my hands.

"No tequila for you."

I flop backwards on the sofa. "Whatever."

Miller slams a bottle of gin on the coffee table. "It's time."

I groan. "We couldn't use a different type of alcohol for truth or punch?"

Truth or punch is a 'game' we play when one of us Bragg brothers is struggling but won't admit what's going on with him. It usually ends up with all of us drunk and one of us bruised.

Miller pours shots and hands each of us one. I sniff the liquid and grimace. I hate gin. Give me tequila any day of the week. Yes, I tend to remove my clothes when I drink tequila. I don't know what the big deal is. Public nudity is not a crime in Winter Falls.

"Truth or punch," Miller growls.

"Truth or punch," I repeat before downing the shot. Ugh. Gross.

"Why is Miller being especially grumpy tonight?" I ask.

He crosses his arms over his chest and looks down at me. "We ask the questions at truth or punch. Not you."

I sigh. "No need for punching. I'll tell you whatever you want to know."

Basically, the game works like this. Whoever's in the hot seat – me in this instance – gets questioned by the others. If he refuses to answer a question, the questioner gets to punch him.

He smirks. "Baby Brody's afraid of being punched."

I hate being called the baby, but I swallow my growl. I know better than to give my brothers ammunition they can use against me when we're playing truth or punch. I've played this game enough in the past year as Riley, Miller, and Elder found their significant others.

"Me first," Peace declares.

I roll my eyes. "Yeah, yeah. We know you're the oldest and get to start the questions."

"Have you told Soleil you love her?"

Elder groans. "You can't ask yes or no questions. It defeats the entire purpose of truth or punch."

"Yes," I answer Peace's initial question before he can formulate a new one, which would be against the rules. Not that anyone cares about the rules.

"What was Soleil's response to your declaration?" Elder asks.

I drink another shot of gin while I formulate my answer. The trick is to answer the question but leave room for misinterpretation.

"She didn't believe me."

"Why not?" Miller grumbles.

"Dude. You're grumpier than grumpy today. Who pissed in your Cheerios?"

"You did."

"I'm positive I would remember weeing in your cereal."

"My fiancée," he begins and I roll my eyes.

He loves to throw the word fiancée around. Good for him. He proposed to Eden and she said yes. Big whoop. It's possible my jealousy is showing. Or I've had too much gin. Either way.

"My fiancée is upset her best friend is hurting."

"It's not my fault."

"My turn," Riley says. "Why isn't it your fault?"

"Hold on. He hasn't answered my question yet," Miller points out.

"Go on." Riley nudges me. "Answer the man's question."

I glare at him. "You're my twin. You're supposed to be on my side."

He snorts. "The same way you were on my side when things with Moon went tits up."

"Not fair. Things with Moon went tits up because you were an idiot. I'm not an idiot. I didn't do anything wrong except love Soleil."

"Why did Soleil break up with you?" Peace asks.

I wag my finger at him. "It's not your turn to ask questions yet."

"I concede my question to him," Riley says.

"Me, too," Miller agrees.

Elder motions toward me. "Go ahead. Answer the question."

"I'm sure you already know the answer. The whole town knows by now. Soleil came home and the fire department was there. She thought I was trying to pull a prank and accidentally started a fire."

Peace shakes his head. "Haven't you learned not to play with fire yet?"

"I wasn't playing with fire. The gossip gals distracted me from my cooking and the croutons burnt. The smoke alarm went off. That's it. End of story."

"Did you tell Soleil this?" Peace asks.

I don't remind him it's not his turn yet. If we do this the proper way, I have to drink a shot for every question posed whether I answer it or not. Considering all the pranks I've played on my brothers, I know better than to be around them when I'm passed out drunk and they're sober.

"She wouldn't let me speak. Seeing River in his fireman gear reminded her of her shed burning down and she freaked."

"I can't blame her there."

Neither can I, which is why I let her kick me out without too much of a fight. She needed to calm down but there was no way in hell I was saying the words 'calm down' in front of her. I'm not an idiot.

"Did you show her the shed?" Elder asks.

"I didn't get the chance."

His brow furrows. "The shed's been done for weeks now."

"I wanted to make it an event. Thus, the fancy dinner."

Riley taps his chin as he studies me. "You're afraid to show her the shed. Why?"

I scowl. "I'm not afraid."

"Yeah, you are. Tell the truth or Miller's punching you."

Miller grins as he cracks his knuckles.

"Now, hold on a minute. These questions and how you've asked them bear no resemblance to truth or punch whatsoever. I'm not letting Miller punch me just because you've decided it's okay."

Peace shrugs. "We're streamlining the process."

"I believe you have the words streamlining and steamrolling confused."

"I don't steamroll people. I interrogate them. If you wish, I can drag you down to the station for an interrogation."

No way in hell is he dragging me to the station. Soleil will get word and call me a child again. Not happening. "On what charges?"

"I'll think of something." He nods toward Miller. "Or you can let him punch you."

"Or you can answer the question." Elder presses a shot glass into my hands.

"This is some bullshit," I mutter before drinking the gin.

"Soleil thinks I don't have any money. She thinks I live off my trust fund. I want her to know I bought the materials with my own money and built the shed with my own hands."

"What does this have to do with you being afraid?" Riley asks.

"She claims I don't have enough money to pay her rent, even though I offered to pay."

"I'm confused. Is anyone else understanding this?" Elder asks.

I jump to my feet. "I want Soleil to know I'm a success. I don't want her to think I'm a trust fund baby."

"Okay. How are you going to become a success?" Riley asks.

"Become a success?" I shout.

His brow furrows. "Um, yeah?"

I pound my chest. "I am a success. I founded a software game company worth millions of dollars. My net worth is more than ten million."

With a start, I realize I'm not lying. My company is a success. And has been for a while. There was no reason to wait to tell my brothers.

"Hold on. I thought you played video games for a living," Riley says.

"Yeah. Don't you play games on behalf of other people who don't have time to get their tokens or whatever it's called?" Elder asks.

"I don't play video games for a living. I develop video games."

Peace scratches his chin. "Why does no one know about this?"

"Because I wanted to wait until I was a success to share it with my brothers. Because I wanted my brothers to be proud of me for a change. Instead of calling me a baby."

"But you are the baby," Elder insists.

"I'm the youngest of the family. I'm not a fucking baby. I'm tired of everyone calling me a child and underestimating me."

"Then, maybe you should show people your bank account," Riley suggests.

"It's not about the money."

"Dude, you're worth ten million. It is about the money."

"Holy crap." Peace holds up his phone. "Have none of you googled your brother before?"

"Give me." Miller snatches the phone from Peace.

Elder reads over Miller's shoulder. "Your company was named as one of the fastest growing software companies last year."

"I'm kind of a genius," I say.

Riley smacks my shoulder. "We know you're a genius."

"It'd be nice if you showed it once in a while instead of treating me like a baby."

"I don't know. If treating you like a baby lit a fire under your ass to create a multi-million dollar company before you hit thirty, then maybe we should call you baby more often," Elder says.

He clears his throat. "How does a woman make a man a millionaire?" He grins. "She marries a billionaire."

"You're not funny," I tell him.

"I'm confused. You're our little brother, the silly prankster," Riley says and I elbow him.

"You're two minutes older than me. The little brother jokes aren't funny anymore."

He holds up his hands. "Still a prankster."

I shrug. "No one took me seriously. You get told something often enough and you start to believe it."

"If you're worried Soleil thinks you're a failure, you should show her your bank account," Elder suggests, and Miller grunts in agreement.

"I don't want her to be with me because of my money."

Peace chuckles. "She was willing to sleep with you when she thought you were penniless. She's clearly not after your money."

Riley rubs his hands together. "We need to come up with a plan for you to get Soleil back. Suggestions, anyone?"

"Not a dinner," Miller grumbles.

"Yeah, big guy. I figured that out for myself."

"This is easy," Peace says. "All he has to do is reveal the pottery shed all ready to be used and they'll be married with two kids in no time."

I don't know about revealing the shed idea, but the idea of being married and having children with Soleil is appealing, very appealing. She's going to be the best mom. And she'll keep me on the straight and narrow when I screw up.

"Ah, look at Brody with the silly smile on his face. It must be love."

I punch Riley before he can duck.

"Ow! Since when does Brody know how to throw a punch?"

I ignore him and the rest of my brothers as they talk trash. I've got plans to make and a woman to win back.

Chapter 36

"HOLD ON," I SAY to the insurance agent.

I drop the phone from my ear to enter my house where no one is cooking dinner or cleaning or playing silly videogames while lounging on the sofa. It feels empty in here. Probably because it is.

My stomach clenches and I rub my hand over it. I can't help smiling. A baby. I'm having a baby. I frown. I need to tell the baby's daddy about his existence.

My phone vibrates in my hand. Oops. I kind of forgot all about the phone call.

"Ms. Hawk. Are you listening to me?" The insurance agent asks.

"I'm sorry. Can you repeat what you said?"

"I'm sorry, Ms. Hawk, but we won't be honoring your claim for the pottery shed."

"What? Why not? I'm paid up on all my insurance premiums."

"As I stated earlier." She clears her throat. "The pottery kiln had a faulty wire."

"I'm aware."

"Since the kiln had been recalled, your insurance claim will not be honored."

"Wait! What? The kiln had been recalled? I never received any notice about it being recalled."

"We consulted the manufacturer and they confirmed they notified all registered owners and placed ads in all pottery trade magazines."

"Pottery trade magazines? I don't subscribe to any pottery trade magazines."

"It's clearly indicated in your insurance policy that in the event an item recalled by the manufacturer is the cause of the damage, the insurance company is not liable to pay the insurance claim."

"Can you send me this in writing?" I ask since I didn't understand ninety-five percent of what she said.

"You should receive written confirmation of our conversation in the mail within a few days. If there's nothing else?" She doesn't wait for me to respond before wishing me a good day and hanging up.

I resist the temptation to throw my telephone across the room. I slam it on the table instead. This is a disaster of epic proportions. How am I going to rebuild the pottery shed without the insurance money? I have some savings but it's not enough to buy a new kiln, let alone build a shed.

And I can't work at the community center forever. I mean I can. They offered me a permanent position as a pottery teacher there. I'm happy to teach some classes but I'm not a teacher. I'm a potter. I need my time at the wheel to create my art unencumbered by students.

What am I going to do? *Think, Soleil. Think.*

Maybe it's not as bad as I'm making it out to be. Maybe the shed isn't completely burned down. Maybe I can rebuild instead of starting over completely. And maybe I've lost my mind. No time like the present to find out how deep the trouble I'm in is.

I march outside and stare at the tarp covering the burned out shed. I've been told to stay away because of the fire investigation but obviously, the investigation is over if the insurance company is denying my claim.

I grab the tarp and pull. Ugh. This is harder than I thought it would be.

"Can I help you, dear?" Petal asks as she joins me.

"I've got this corner," Feather calls as she grabs hold of the other corner of the tarp.

I glance around me to find all of the gossip gals standing in my backyard.

"What are you doing here?"

"We came to check on you. We heard about what happened with Brody," Sage says.

As if me discussing my love life with the gossip gals is ever going to happen.

"You weren't spying on me?" I point to the binoculars around Clove's neck. "You better put those away before Peace sees them."

"I've been bird watching," she claims.

I snort. "Bird watching? Is that what we're calling it these days?"

"I love bird watching," Cayenne chimes in.

None of the gossip gals have been bird watching a day in their lives. They've been snooping on the residents of Winter Falls with those binoculars, but there's no use arguing with them. Despite their advanced years, none of them have learned to concede an argument even when it's obvious they're losing.

"As long as you're here, can you help me get this tarp off?"

Sage immediately starts ordering everyone around. "Feather you take the far corner. Petal, the closest corner. Cayenne and Clove in the middle."

I step back and let them do their thing. My back is killing me from sitting at my wheel all day. If they want to do the heavy lifting, they can be my guest.

"One, two, three – heave!" Sage shouts. I wouldn't be surprised if she pulled a whip out and started cracking it. "And again."

I'm confused as to why removing the tarp is this much work. Was the pottery shed not burned to the ground? Do I have a structure I can rebuild on?

The gossip gals whoop as the tarp falls off the shed. The shed? I rub my eyes to clear my vision but I'm not imagining things. There is a brand-new shed where my old shed used to be.

"What's happening here?" Am I having a fever dream? I pinch myself. "Ow." Definitely awake. But still confused as to what's happening here.

"Oh. Wow. It's gorgeous. I've been dying to see it," Sage says.

My confusion isn't clearing up any. "Dying to see it? You knew about this?"

"The whole town did."

I press my fingers against my temples where I feel a headache coming on. Maybe this is one of those super realistic dreams. Maybe the insurance company didn't phone and deny my claim. And maybe—

Sage grasps my arm and drags me closer to the building. "Touch it. It's real."

I don't know what's worse. Sage knowing I'm having a difficult time with reality at the moment or standing in front of the gossip gals caressing the wall of my new pottery shed.

My new pottery shed. Holy cows have come home! I have a new pottery shed.

"Did the whole town get together and construct this shed for me?"

Winter Falls is awesome this way. If a neighbor is going through a rough time, she's not going through it alone or for long.

"No, we didn't," Sage says.

"But we would have," Feather adds.

Petal nods. "If necessary."

"I would have supplied the coffee and cookies," Clove says.

Cayenne stretches her arms above her head before reaching down to touch her toes. I wish I could touch my toes. "And I would have helped with stretching before and after any strenuous activity."

"If the town didn't do this, who did?"

Sage clears her throat. "We're not allowed to say."

I cock a brow and wait. Sage and the gossip gals have never been able to keep a secret before. When she doesn't immediately cave, I cross my arms over my chest and tap my toe. "I'm waiting."

"I don't know what for. I can keep a secret."

I snort. "Sure, you can."

She wags her finger. "You're not going to get me to spill a secret just to prove I can keep a secret."

She's confusing me, so I focus my attention on Feather.

"Next month's smutty book is *Make Me Yours* by Melanie Harlow," she blurts out.

"I thought we were saving the single father book for December," Petal says.

"No." Feather shakes her head. "We need to start in November. December's too far away."

"I guess I better start a new batch of candles."

"What are you talking about?" I yell. "The smutty book club has nothing to do with my shed."

Clove pats my hand. "Of course, not, dear."

Cayenne scratches her neck. "What was the question again?"

I point at them. "To think I defended the lot of you when Brody badmouthed you."

Sage gasps. "Brody badmouthed us?"

"He blamed you for the fire in the house."

Clove's nose scrunches. "He's not exactly wrong. If we hadn't distracted him, he never would have burned the croutons."

"I may have phoned River a bit prematurely. But he's just so dang sexy in his fireman uniform. I can't resist him." Petal winks.

"You're happily married," I remind her.

"Orion and I have an understanding. I can look as long as I don't touch."

"What about pinching?" I ask her. "I've seen you pinch plenty of young man's buts."

She waves away my question. "Pinching does not count as touching."

"I beg to differ," Brody says as he strolls into the backyard.

I study him. He doesn't appear to be heartbroken. Jerk. He should be devastated I broke up with him and kicked him out. It's the least he could do.

"What are you doing here?" I ask. "I told you to come get your stuff when I'm at work."

"I'm not picking up my stuff."

I cross my arms over my chest. "Well, I'm not packing it up for you. If you don't come get it, I'm throwing it all away."

He growls. "I'm not here to discuss my stuff."

His gaze dips to my stomach and I place a hand over it. Shit. Does he know? Who told?

Chapter 37

BRODY

Soleil placing a protective hand over her stomach is the confirmation I need. She's pregnant and she didn't tell me. I ignore the hurt gathering in a ball in my chest. There'll be time for hurt later. Soleil and I have things to discuss first.

"Is there something you have to tell me?"

She points to the pottery shed. "Is there something *you* have to tell me?"

Clove claps. "This is good. Front row seats."

"Too bad we don't have popcorn," Sage complains.

Petal sighs. "Project Cub is my favorite!"

Feather rolls her eyes. "You say that about every project. They can't all be your favorites."

"I don't know why not."

I inhale a deep breath before I snap at the gossip gals. I owe them. I eavesdropped on their conversation before I made my appearance known. They kept my secret about the shed.

Therefore, no yelling at the crazy old ladies today. Also, no referring to them as crazy old ladies out loud.

"Ahem. Ladies."

Sage bats her eyelashes at me. "Yes, Brody."

"Can I speak to Soleil alone?"

"We're not stopping you."

Soleil grabs my hand and drags me toward the shed. "We need to leave since they never will."

I don't say anything since she's not wrong. Instead, I open the shed door and usher her inside. She gasps and drops my hand to survey the room. She runs her hands over the new kiln and pottery wheel.

"I can't believe this. It's incredible." She frowns when she notices the rows of finished pottery on the shelves. "What are those doing there? I thought none of my pots survived the fire."

"They didn't. Those are some of your new pots."

Her brow wrinkles. "Some of my new pots? But I haven't had any time to build up any stock."

I shrug.

Her jaw drops when she connects the dots. "You're J. Smith. You're the one who's been ordering the most expensive pieces I have listed online."

"Guilty as charged."

"You couldn't have thought of a more original name?"

"Fooled you, didn't I?"

She growls. Shit. I said the wrong thing.

"Ignore what I said. I'm an idiot."

She snorts. "You won't hear me arguing with you."

I wish she would never argue with me again, but I know couples argue. Now to convince her to be a couple with me again.

"Is there something you need to tell me?" I nod toward her stomach.

She wags her finger at me. "I'm not done yelling at you about the pottery shed."

"Why yelling? I thought you'd be happy I built you the shed."

"You built this shed?"

I hold up my hands. "With my very own hands. I used Riley's tools, though."

"But how did you afford this?"

Crap. I knew I'd have to tell her about my company and the money, but I thought I could tell her after we reconciled. There goes my plan. I grasp her hands and lead her to a chair.

"I need to sit down for this? Oh boy."

I pace the shed as I consider how to tell her the truth. I should have prepared myself for this. I knew the question would come up.

"I have money," I blurt out.

"Oookay?"

"I don't play video games, I develop them."

I pause and she motions for me to continue.

"I actually have my own software company."

Her mouth drops open. "You have your own company?"

I nod. "And it's going quite well."

Her mouth snaps shut and she narrows her eyes on me. "Define quite well."

My cheeks warm. "It's a multi-million dollar company."

"Then, you're rich?"

"Some would say that."

"What would you say?"

My cheeks are feeling hot now. "I'm a millionaire."

"You're a millionaire!" she shouts. "And no one knew?"

"We knew!" Sage yells through the window.

Soleil springs to her feet and stomps to the door. I catch her before she can open it. "I'll go deal with them. Don't upset the baby."

Her shoulders sag. "You know?"

I nod. "Be right back."

I stand in the backyard and confront the gossip gals. "How much to get you to go away and give us some privacy?"

"Are you going to get busy?" Feather asks.

"I could use some inspiration," Petal adds.

"How much?" I ask again because I am not discussing sex with a bunch of women old enough to be my grandmother.

"A donation to restore the gazebo in the town square." Sage hands me a piece of paper. "Here's the information."

I'm glad this woman is on my side. She'd be a formidable opponent. I wait until Sage herds the group away before returning to the shed.

"You know?" Soleil asks again as soon as the door is shut behind me.

I nod.

"Who told?"

"Does it matter?"

"Yes," she grits out. "My former friends promised to keep my pregnancy a secret. I need to know who to kill."

I scratch the back of my neck. "You're not going to be happy."

She crosses her arms over her chest. "Do I appear happy to you now?"

Since she's spitting fire from her eyeballs, I'd say no.

I lean against the prep table next to her chair. "They all told."

"What?"

"Moon, Eden, and Harmony came to me as a group."

"No Ashlyn? Huh. Maybe she can keep a secret."

"They're worried about you."

"They should be worried about themselves when I get ahold of them." She shakes her fist in the air.

I grasp her fist and lace my fingers through hers. When she doesn't protest, hope soars through me. Maybe all is not lost.

"You're pregnant?" She nods. "With my baby?"

She glares at me. "Yes."

I grin. "How far along are you? Do we want to know if it's a boy or a girl? I have some ideas for names."

Her brow wrinkles. "You sound excited."

"Because I am. The woman I love is having my baby. What's not to be excited about?"

"We broke up."

"A temporary issue."

She yanks her hand from mine. "A temporary issue? How is our break-up a temporary issue? You tried to burn my house down."

I kneel in front of her. "I didn't try to burn your house down and you know it." She sniffs and lifts her nose in the air. "I know you're scared. Having a baby is scary."

"I'm not scared of having this baby. I can't wait to have this baby."

"Then, what are you afraid of?"

"Nothing."

I cock a brow. "Nothing? Soleil Hawk is afraid of nothing in this world. Not losing her house. Not becoming a parent. Nothing."

She shoves me but I refuse to budge.

"Stop being a dork."

"But you love this dork."

Crap. Crap. Crap. I didn't mean to say that. But now the words are out there, I'm going with it. Go big or go home. What about going big to go home?

"It's why you're scared. Love scares the crap out of you."

"I don't want to lose you."

"So, you pushed me away first?"

"It's better than watching you wither and die in front of me."

"I'm not going to wither and die in front of you."

She slaps my shoulder. "You can't know that! You can't predict the future!" she shouts and promptly bursts into tears.

I gather her in my arms and carry her out of the shed to the house where I sit on the couch with her in my lap.

"Stupid pregnancy hormones. Making me cry," she mumbles as she brushes the tears from her eyes.

"Hmm… Okay…Let's blame the pregnancy." I take over wiping the tears from her face.

"You better believe your fine ass I'll be blaming the pregnancy for everything for the next seven months so get used to it."

I smile. "As long as I'm around you, I don't care if you blame vampires on your moods."

She rolls her eyes. "Everyone knows vampires aren't real. Shifters on the other hand…"

"Are you done avoiding the subject now?"

"What subject?"

"Obviously not," I mutter before continuing in a normal voice, "Me, you, us, the baby, your love for me."

"You really love me?"

"How could I not? You're perfect. It's why I lied about being allergic to dogs to force you to let me live here."

"You lied about being allergic to dogs?" She shakes her head. "Why am I not surprised?"

Her resignation changes to ire and she glares at me. "If you say you ruined your bed on purpose, I'm going to slice your balls off and feed them to Harmony's dogs."

I cringe. "I was actually trying to prepare a July 4th surprise for you."

"Dang it. You make it hard for me to be mad at you."

I smirk. "Good. I hope you feel the same when we're eighty and rocking on our rocking chairs on the porch and I decide to throw water balloons at the grandkids."

"You really are okay with me being pregnant."

"Why do you sound surprised? I'm not a child."

"Whoa. I didn't say you were." She pauses. "This time."

"Good. Are you over the whole I'm too old for you bullshit?"

She scrunches her nose and I can't resist kissing the tip. She's adorable.

"I'm trying. I kind of got stuck on my dad being younger than my mom."

"I'm not your dad."

"I know. It's just…" She blows out a breath. "The way he left everything to me when Mom was sick. It's not easy to forget."

I kiss her nose. "You don't need to forget. But you do need to remember I'm not him. And, if you need a reminder, I'll help you."

"Let me guess. By doing a prank."

I puff out my chest. "What can I say? My pranks are the best cheer her up medicine."

She giggles. "You always make me laugh. No wonder I love you." She slams a hand over her mouth.

I kiss her forehead before prying her hands away. "I love you, too, pixie girl."

"We're having a baby."

I nod. "Yep. We're having a baby. And I'm moving back in."

"Who says?"

"If you think I'm going to let you live alone when you're pregnant with my baby, you're sorely mistaken. I plan to be here every step of the way."

"Even when my ankles are swollen to the size of my knees?"

"I'll massage them before running you a bath."

"You're perfect."

I grin. "I know. Glad you finally figured it out."

"Dork."

"Your dork. Forever and ever."

"I've never been this happy. I'm terrified."

"Ride the wave with me, pixie girl. Ride the wave."

She blows out a breath. "Okay. I hope you have a surfboard for me and the baby."

I have something for her all right. I meld my lips to hers and she sighs. I push my way inside. I can finally breathe again. Having Soleil in my arms, smelling her scent, tasting her luscious mouth is where I belong. Where I will always belong.

Chapter 38

NOVEMBER

"I don't know about this," I say as I survey the house all decorated for the party. "It's too early for a baby shower."

Brody frowns. "Why is it too early? Are you worried? Have you not been feeling well? Do we need to go to the doctor?"

I hold up my palm. "Stop."

He's become Mr. Overprotective since we got back together. He even bought an electric car to drive me to doctor's appointments and in case of emergencies.

He catches my wrist and kisses my palm. "Are you feeling okay?"

He's also become Mr. Attentive since he found out about the pregnancy. He pours me baths, rubs my feet, and makes dinner every night. A girl could get used to this. I'm enjoying it while I can because I know everything will change once the baby arrives.

I rub my baby bump. "I'm feeling perfect."

He leans over to speak to my belly. "Did you hear that, baby Anakin? Momma thinks you're perfect."

I ignore how squishy his speaking to the baby makes me feel and smack the top of his head. "We are not naming our baby after a character in Star Wars."

"Why not?"

"Maybe because Anakin becomes Darth Vader."

"Then, you're open to other Star Wars names? But not those who go to the dark side?"

"That's not what I said."

"It's what I heard. I'll make a list."

"You're trying to get my mind off my worry about the party, aren't you?"

He grins. "And it worked. I'm a genius."

"You're a dork."

He kisses my nose. "I'm your dork and you're my pixie girl."

I don't want sweet kisses on the nose. I grasp his sweater and haul him close. I push up on my tiptoes and bite his lower lip.

He growls. "You'll pay for that later."

"Yes, please."

"Troublemaker," he mumbles before licking my bottom lip.

"Your troublemaker."

"You trying to get me all hot and bothered before my entire family shows up?"

"I vote for hot and bothered. Forget about the family."

He sighs before wrapping his arms around me and swaying me from side to side. "The baby shower is going to be great."

"It's too early for a baby shower," I whine.

"Why? You're in your second trimester and everyone in town knows you're pregnant anyway. We might as well have the party now." The doorbell rings. "Too late now anyway."

"I'll get it," I say, but Brody pushes past me to open the door.

"I'm pregnant. My legs work fine," I tell him but he ignores me. Mr. Overprotective has arrived at the party. Awesome.

"Riley. Moon." He motions them inside. "Please, come in."

"Told you they'd answer the door," Moon says.

Riley shrugs. "I thought they'd ignore us and continue making out."

"Were you watching us through the window?" I ask Moon.

"Your window is right there. It's kind of impossible not to notice."

I wave a fist at her. "If you stepped in my bushes, I'll ruin you."

She lifts the platters she's holding. "I guess you don't want any cake or cookies."

"I'll take those." Brody grabs the platters while giving his twin the stink eye. "You couldn't carry these for your girlfriend?"

Moon frowns. "I don't let him carry anything, the little thief."

Riley puffs up his chest. "I'm not little."

"Fine. You big thief."

"What'd he do now?" I ask.

"He snuck out of bed in the middle of the night to eat half a dozen of the cookies I made for today."

Riley grins. "I'm a growing boy. I need to be fed."

Moon smacks his middle. "You're going to get fat if you keep it up."

He wiggles his eyebrows. "Good thing I know how to burn off the calories."

She marches to the dining area where the food is set up. "I can't with him," she mumbles as she begins to rearrange the food to her liking. "I just can't."

There's a knock on the door, so I leave her to it to answer it. Brody drapes an arm over my shoulders. I guess we're answering the door together.

Elder enters holding Robin in his arms with Harmony trailing him.

I hold out my hands. "I want a cuddle."

Elder hands me Robin without any fuss. I kiss her forehead before reading her t-shirt. "World's best cousin."

I giggle and Elder snatches the baby back. "You saw the t-shirt. She's mine now." He's such a baby hog.

"Oh my gosh! You popped!" Harmony points to my belly.

I turn to the side and strike a pose allowing my baby bump to be seen. Harmony hugs me. "I'm so excited for you."

"Because you think we'll alternate babysitting the babies."

"Excellent idea!" Ashlyn shouts as she arrives with Patience on her hip. Rowan grunts. "Big guy agrees. We'll make a babysitting pool."

"What's all the excitement?" Eden asks. "Are you building a pool?"

I glance over at Brody and notice the sparkle in his eyes. I wag a finger at him. "No."

"But what if I build a community pool? Winter Falls doesn't have one."

"We have the river where people can swim."

He shivers. "The river is freezing cold. And it has a current. I don't want little Kylo to be in any danger."

"Kylo?" Eden glances back and forth between me and Brody. "You're naming your child after a Star Wars character?"

Moon claps. "It's a boy! How exciting?"

"Everyone hold on before the rumors start flowing," I have to shout to make myself heard over the crowd. "One, we don't know the sex of the baby." I glare at Brody. "And, two, we are not naming our child after a bad guy in Star Wars."

"Of course not," Sage says as she bustles inside with Clove, Cayenne, Petal, and Feather hot on her heels. "You'll give the baby a good Winter Falls name."

"What's a good Winter Falls name?" Brody asks before I can stop him.

"Aderyn, Enara, Sparrow, Drake, Teal, Lark, Starling, Wren. I'll make you a list," Feather says.

"No," Cayenne grumbles. "You will not win this bet by cheating."

Brody leans over to whisper a question in my ear. "What bet?"

I elbow him. "You know darn well everyone in town is betting on the birthdate and name of our baby."

He smirks. "Why do you think I keep making Star Wars references?"

"You're a genius."

He tweaks my nose. "Which is what I've been trying to tell you."

"I'm certain we can figure out a Star Wars name that meets Winter Falls' criteria," I say to the crowd.

Feather nods. "I'll get on it. Gratitude at the library will help."

I giggle. The librarian won't be any help since she can't resist a good bet.

Brody kisses my temple. "Told you the party would be fun."

"I didn't say it wouldn't be fun. I said…" I trail off because I can't remember why I was nervous about the party.

Daisy rushes into the house. "I can't believe this. Why would he do this? Why wouldn't he tell me?"

Her fiancé Lennon chases after her. "Petal, I'm certain he has a reasonable explanation."

She glares at him. "Siding with the man, are you?"

To his credit, Lennon doesn't run away. He captures her hands and draws her near. "I'm on your side. Always and forever."

"What's going on? Why is Mom freaked out?" Elder glares at Brody. "What did you do?"

"Why are you accusing me? I didn't do anything."

"You didn't switch out all my underwear to a smaller size?"

I slap my hand over my mouth before my giggle can escape. It was beyond hilarious watching Elder walk around with underwear too tight on. Forest even took him aside to promote the value of going bottomless while Miller tried to convince him to go commando.

"You shouldn't have told Soleil about the car I bought for her. It was supposed to be a surprise."

Peace arrives, scans the room, and marches to the brothers. He forces his way in between Brody and Elder. "Enough. Trust me. You have other things to worry about."

He nods toward the door. Everyone in the room turns to watch as Damon walks inside with a small girl hoisted on his hip and holding Love Hill's hand.

"Go on. No one's going to bite you," he encourages Love Hill.

"About damn time," Brody says.

Elder glares at him. "You knew about this?"

Brody snorts. "As if you can keep a secret from me."

"Welp. I guess we can add Damon's name to the babysitting pool," Ashlyn announces.

Chapter 39

No one's going to welcome me with open arms? ~ Message from Love Hill on the Winter Falls Facebook page

LOVE HILL

"There," I say as I finish braiding Skye's hair.

"I'm a princess," she says as she twists her head back and forth to flick her braids.

"You are." I nod.

Skye is literally the most adorable child to walk the earth. From her blonde curly hair to the freckles covering her face – adorable.

"Thank you, Nanny Love."

She's also the sweetest, most polite child in the world.

Damon walks into the room and I ignore the way my stomach dips and my heart rate increases. He's off limits. He's my employer and the father of this wonderful child in my care.

"Are you ready, sweetheart?"

Skye jumps off the bed and runs to him. "I'm ready, Daddy!" She lifts her arms and he immediately picks her up and twirls her around.

I swallow my sigh as I watch how wonderful a father Damon is with Skye. For someone who had a five-year-old dumped on his doorstep a few months ago, he's taken to fatherhood like it's his calling.

"How about you, LH? Are you ready?" Damon asks.

"Me?" I point to myself. "I'm not going to the party."

"Yes, you are."

I stand and back away with my hands raised. "I didn't agree to this."

He frowns. "You agreed to be my in-home nanny and care for my child. I need you to care for my child."

"But you'll be with her at the party. It seems a bit ostentatious to bring me as well."

I'm not only refusing to go because it's a party in Winter Falls where everyone hates me. I do believe what I'm saying. Bringing a nanny to a party is a bit over the top.

"My brothers are going to discover I have a child for the first time. I don't want Skye to be forgotten about while I deal with their bullsh— bologna."

Fiddlesticks. He's right. Damon has kept the existence of Skye a secret from his family for the past few months. They are going to lose their minds when they find out.

"Fine. I don't like it. But fine."

"Yeah!" Skye cheers. "Nanny Love is coming to the party."

"Are you ready to leave?" Damon asks me.

"I need a minute to prepare Skye's bag."

"We'll wait outside by the car."

I wait until the door closes behind him before collapsing on the bed. This is bad. No, not bad. Bad isn't a strong enough word to convey what a shit show this is going to be.

The people of Winter Falls are going to lose their ever-loving minds when they discover I'm the caretaker for Damon's daughter. I'm going to lose my job. I clutch my chest as fear rolls through me.

I wish I was exaggerating. I admit I'm prone to dramatics but in this case, I'm not being a drama queen. I wouldn't put it past Sage to call child services to have me banned from ever being in Skye's presence again. This day sucks.

But I'm not going to hide in this bedroom all scared. Been there. Done that. Didn't help the situation one iota.

I stand and march to the suitcase in the corner of the bedroom. We're staying in a hotel in White Bridge, one town over from Winter Falls, while Damon gets up the courage to tell his family about Skye. Is it wrong to wish he didn't find the courage? Probably.

I put together a bag of essentials before squaring my shoulders and walking out of the room to the parking lot. Damon already has Skye strapped in the back seat when I arrive.

"There's no reason to be stressed," he says as he accepts the bag from me and places it in the trunk. "My brothers are assholes, but they won't run you out of town."

I'm not worried about his brothers. I force a smile and nod before settling in the passenger seat for the thirty-minute drive to Winter Falls.

Neither of us speaks during the drive. It's not awkward, though, as Skye prattles away from the backseat. She doesn't appear to notice our lack of response.

"Where does Soleil live?" Damon asks when we arrive in Winter Falls.

"Turn left here," I say as I direct him to the house where his brother Brody and his girlfriend are having a baby shower. I inhale a deep breath to center myself. *It's not a big deal, Love. People have babies all the time. Just not me. Never me.*

We park across the street from Soleil's house. My hands tremble as I release my seatbelt. Fortunately, Damon doesn't notice as he's already up and out of the car to help Skye.

He opens my door and holds out his hand. "Come on. We'll do this together."

I grasp his hand like it's a lifeline. We don't make it two steps before his mom, Daisy, rushes toward us.

"Damon! I didn't expect you." Her brow furrows as she realizes he's not alone. "With a small child and woman. What's going on?"

"Mom," he greets and kisses her cheek. He nods to his mom's fiancé. "Lennon."

"What's going on?" she repeats her question.

"I'll explain everything inside."

"You'll explain everything this minute."

"I don't want to tell the story multiple times."

Lennon nudges her. "He's right, Petal. Let's go inside where he can explain everything."

She growls at him. "You're siding with him?" She huffs and rushes inside the house with him chasing after her.

"This is going to be fun," Damon mumbles.

"It's a party, Daddy. Parties are fun," Skye explains.

He tweaks her nose. "Yes, they are, baby girl."

I clutch his hand as we walk toward the house.

"Go on. No one's going to bite you," he encourages at the doorway and I step inside the house with him.

"About damn time," Brody says.

Elder glares at him. "You knew about this?"

Brody snorts. "As if you can keep a secret from me."

"Welp. I guess we can add Damon's name to the babysitting pool," Ashlyn announces.

"I have some explaining to do," Damon begins.

Chapter 40

BRODY

I hear the vacuum cleaner running as I step onto the porch and sigh. Soleil shouldn't be cleaning in her condition. But I know better than to say anything.

I already made that mistake once. Never again. Being chased by a pregnant woman with a broom is not on my list of adventures I want to repeat.

"Soleil!" I greet when I open the door.

She switches off the vacuum and wipes a hand over her brow. I frown. She's sweating. She shouldn't be sweating. She should be relaxing.

"How are you and little Palpatine doing today?"

She scowls at me. "We are not naming our child Palpatine."

At least it's our child today. An improvement over yesterday when it was my child since she had indigestion and couldn't sleep.

"But we can use the nickname Palpy."

She shivers. "It reminds me of pap smear. No."

"I'll work on it."

"No, you won't. You'll review the list of names I made and choose the three you prefer."

"I reviewed the list. It was boring."

"Boring?" She raises her eyebrows. "Callista is boring?"

"Yep."

"Leaf is boring?"

I feign gagging. "Not boring but the poor kid would be bullied."

She throws her arms in the air. "Are you deliberately trying to annoy me?"

I grin. "What happens if I say yes? Are you going to chase me with a broom again?"

"Maybe I should use a knife this time."

"Bloodthirsty. I love it."

She rolls her eyes. "You're crazy. And you're driving me crazy."

"It wasn't a very long drive."

"Enough with this." She motions to the hallway. "I want you to clean out your office. I need to get the baby's room ready. It should be done already."

"Why already? You're not due for another two months."

"I don't want to be moving furniture when I'm as big as a house."

I growl. "As if I'd let you move furniture."

"Great. You're here now and can help."

When she smiles, I realize I've been had. What she doesn't realize is there's a great big surprise for her behind the door.

"How about I clean out my office tomorrow while you're working? You don't need to help."

She crosses her arms over her chest. "Really? You're going to clean it out tomorrow? How many times have you told me you'd clean out your office already?"

I scratch my chin and pretend to think about it. "Once?"

"Try thirteen million."

"Pixie girl, I love you to death." Her eyes go soft and I pause to appreciate the moment. "But we both know I'm the mathematical genius in the family."

"Someone thinks awful highly of himself."

"When the algorithm fits." I shrug.

"I hate algorithms," she mutters.

"Don't be a math hater."

"Easy for you to say. The Facebook algorithm didn't decide the only thing you want to read about on your feed is pregnancies."

"I don't understand the problem."

"You wouldn't. Mr. Checked Every Book About Pregnancy Out from the library and asked the librarian if she could order more."

"I want to be prepared." At least she doesn't know about all the childrearing books I've been reading. I may be slightly terrified I'll screw our child up. My mom rocked as a parent, but I didn't exactly have a great example in my dad.

"Enough stalling." She points to the hallway. "Time to enter the dungeon."

"My office is not a dungeon," I grumble but I grasp her hand and draw her down the hallway to the room formerly known as my office.

"I don't understand why you need an office in our house as well as an office at the community center," Soleil complains. She doesn't give me a chance to respond before babbling on, "And how many computers does one man need?"

"You crossed the line," I growl. "You can complain about whatever you want but never say I have too many computers."

She giggles. "You're such a dork."

"I'm a genius dork who loves you." I pull her close to kiss her forehead. "Please don't be mad."

"I'm not going to be mad." She inhales a deep breath. "I'm prepared for the mess."

She's not prepared but she'll see why in a minute. "Maybe I should cover your eyes just in case the view overwhelms you."

"You're extra dorky today."

I bow. "Thank you."

I cover her eyes with my hand before opening the door. I nudge her inside and lift my hands. "Tada!"

"I don't know why you're tada—" She gasps. "Holy cow. When did this happen?"

"I've been working on the nursery for over a month now."

She walks to the crib and runs her hand over the smooth wood. "This is the most gorgeous crib I've ever seen. Are these little pottery wheels carved into the wood?"

"Yes, and little computer screens." I tap one.

"Did you make this?"

I chuckle. "Sorry, but no. The pottery shed was the limit of my construction capabilities. I asked Riley to make it."

"Riley is an artist with wood." She sighs as she continues to run her hands over the crib. "Our child won't know whether to be a potter or a computer geek."

I puff out my chest. "I prefer the word computer genius."

She rolls her eyes.

"Maybe our child will be neither. Our child can be anything he wants to be."

She rubs her hand over her belly. "What if it's a girl?"

"Then, I'll buy a shotgun to warn off all the boys."

"No, I mean you want a boy. Will you be happy with a girl?"

"I don't want a boy."

"But you're always coming up with boy names."

"Because most of the bad guys in Star Wars are men."

She looks to the ceiling as if to ask for patience. She won't find any there. "Again, with the Star Wars."

I pull her into my arms. "Don't act as if you're annoyed with me. I know you love me."

"I can love you and still be annoyed with you at the same time. I'm a woman. I know how to multi-task."

I run my nose along hers. "But you're not annoyed. You're pretending."

"I am a bit annoyed." I cock an eyebrow. "I wanted to get the nursery ready but you already did everything."

I grin.

She narrows her eyes. "What are you grinning about?"

"Ashlyn warned me about the nesting."

"Ashlyn? It wasn't one of the million pregnancy books?"

"I plead the fifth." I retreat a step and grasp her hand to lead her to the closet. "I left this to you."

I open the door and she gasps at the stacks of gift wrapped packages before tugging her hand free from mine. "I need to sort this out."

I wrap my arms around her back and lay my chin on her shoulder. "Do you like your surprise?"

She shrugs. "It's okay."

I whirl her around to face me. "You're full of doggy doo-doo, pixie."

"Okay. Fine." She huffs. "It's a good gift."

"I love how thankful you always are with my gifts."

"I figure if I sound ungrateful at some point, you'll stop spending all of your money on me."

I chuckle. "I'm not spending all of my money on you. I have some left over for the baby."

"And the Olympic-sized pool for Winter Falls."

I may have gotten carried away with the pool situation. But who doesn't want slides and diving boards at their town pool? No one, that's who.

"And the car."

I place a finger over her lips. "We agreed you can't complain about the car since we need one in case of emergencies."

"I'm surprised you don't have an emergency plan for all contingencies."

My cheeks warm.

"You do have an emergency plan!"

"So, sue me. I never want the woman I love or our child to be in danger."

"You're going to be a great dad."

"And you're going to be the best mom ever."

Her smile is wobbly. "I had a great teacher."

"And we'll tell our child all about his *or her* grandmother."

"My mom would have loved grandchildren."

I pull her closer to me. Or, at least, as close as she can get with her pregnant belly. I wipe a stray tear from her cheek. "Don't cry. Please don't cry. Or I'll be forced to buy you a gift to cheer you up."

She slaps my shoulder. "Ever since you admitted you're a millionaire, you've become a menace."

I waggle my eyebrows. "The good kind of menace?"

"Sure. Whatever."

"Burning the bed in the spare bedroom was the best decision I ever made in my life."

She glares at me. "You said it was an accident."

"My statement stands. I love you, pixie girl."

"And, despite my better judgment, I love you, dork."

I touch my lips to hers. I want to throw her over my shoulder and carry her to the bedroom but she shoves me away.

"Now, get out of here. I need to unpack these boxes and put things in their proper place. You probably didn't use a system when you designed the nursery."

I chuckle as I sit in the rocking chair to observe her. I can't get enough of watching Soleil while she's pregnant. If she'll let me, I'll give her a whole soccer team of children.

About the Author

D.E. Haggerty is an American who has spent the majority of her adult life abroad. She has lived in Istanbul, various places throughout Germany, and currently finds herself in The Hague. She has been a military policewoman, a lawyer, a B&B owner/operator and now a writer.